The Golden Heart Series
Book One

THE SECRET
OF THE
GOLDEN HEART

DEBBIE ERICKSON

Dori —

—To a new friendship
—I hope lasts forever!

Love,

Debbie Erickson
Merry Christmas!

First, I give God the glory for going before me and keeping the candle lit on my path, and for giving me the perseverance to finish this story.

Second, I'm grateful to my husband for his love, for being unselfish with my time, and giving me the freedom to make one of my dreams come true.

Third, I dedicate this story to my grandchildren who have inspired me to write it. I leave them with something lasting through the written word.

Every child is unique, even the unborn, and they deserve the best example we can give them. I want to give them hope for the future, to inspire them to discover their true passion, to strive for their dreams, and to never, ever give up.

Printed in the United States of America

ISBN 13: 978-1-5194-3686-3
ISBN 10: 1519436866

Cover Design by Heather McCorkle
http://heathermccorkle.wix.com/mccorklecreations

Editor – Jeni Chappelle
http://www.jenichappelle.com

www.debbie-erickson.com

twitter @Erickson_D

Though this is a work of fiction, although the author holds her beliefs of faith that is portrayed throughout this story. *"So then, faith cometh by hearing, and hearing by the word of God."* ~ Romans 10:17 (NAS)

ONE

Kristian took a deep breath as he peered over the one hundred and thirty foot drop behind Split Rock Lighthouse in Two Harbors, Minnesota. Had his dad met his fate here or in the forest?

Waves from Lake Superior crashed against the cliff, shooting water into the air. The wind whipped his hair and sent shivers across his skin. He wiped his face and continued down the worn path toward the forest. He tugged on his backpack and zipped his jacket until it hugged his neck. He shouldn't have bolted out of the house, but Gracie left him no choice. She always thought she knew best, which always caused fights. It was either fight or flight.

He stopped at the forest's edge and looked up at the Scots pines. They looked like giant, alien soldiers. Jagged shadows from the trees stretched across the glen as the orange curvature of the sun disappeared from sight. Treetops silhouetted against the blueberry sky and twinkling stars. The wet, woodsy scent rushed up his nose. Waves crashed louder as the wind picked up.

A limb cracked and crashed to the ground. He took a deep breath and tightened his grip on the dented, metal flashlight. His dog, Nick, licked his cheek. Kristian flicked the switch, and sprayed the cone-shaped light across the ground as he crept closer toward the forest—if he could only find a clue to his dad's disappearance.

He swallowed hard and went in. Limbs crackled as he tiptoed down the overgrown path. Stewart River ran through the forest on the east. He shone the light and noticed a torn piece of paper on the worn path. He picked it up. Another limb snapped. He shoved the note into his pocket and scanned the area. Several more yards in he froze.

Alon, the ancient oak tree—the forest's primeval icon—loomed. Its dark, edgy streaks wound around its bare, twisted trunk, forming black-eyed knots that stared through the shadows with contempt. Its branches sprawled over the forest canopy like mummy fingers, but it was the huge black hole in its trunk that still stirred embers around his nerves, even after all these years.

Nick nuzzled his wet snout against his neck. Another branch snapped and toppled through the trees. The dog yelped. Kristian twitched. He grasped the dog's snout and hushed him. He could feel the Nick's quick heartbeats against his other hand and his hot breath on his cheek.

A shadow swooped down in a black, smoky haze, and then shot back up through the trees. Its snake-like tail swirled around treetops and vanished. Kristian trembled. He couldn't turn back.

He flicked the light across the ground, scooting wet leaves away with his foot as he scuffled through the debris. He saw no signs of a struggle. He dropped Nick to the ground and tip-toed farther down the path, sweeping wispy vines out of his way, flicking his eyes back and forth for clues.

Nick barked. Kristian froze. Shivers raced up his back when his eyes locked onto Alon's monstrous opening, with its hollowed darkness. The dog darted ahead and disappeared beneath the undergrowth.

"Nick," Kristian whispered loudly, "get back here."

A loud swoosh stirred some leaves.

He clicked the flashlight off, squatted beside some scrub trees, and swallowed so hard he thought he'd swallowed his tongue.

The dog squealed.

"Nick?" Kristian glanced up. A shadowy creature, one his family had failed to convince him was only a legend, slithered around Alon's trunk like a python. Racing back through the spindly vines, Nick barked so quick that his barks caught in his throat before he could take a breath.

"Nick, good, boy. Come on."

Nick leaped into his arms and landed with a garbled grunt. Kristian hobbled past the thin limbs that stung his face like paper cuts. His foot ached and burned as if someone was squeezing the life from it. Then it went numb, and he tripped and rolled beneath an overgrown bush.

The ground squished beneath him. The cool moisture soaked through his pants. He grabbed his foot and muttered, "I hate you."

Nick yelped. He grasped his dog's snout and hushed him again. A chill seized his neck like icy fingers—the shadow's presence. He took a deep, silent breath and held it as a green eye twitched through the trees. He prayed the shadow wouldn't sense them.

Just when he thought he'd pass out from fright, the shadow swooshed into the forest, leaving behind an odor of spoiled meat. When he released Nick's snout, the dog thrashed his tongue across Kristian's mouth and wagged his tail.

"It's okay, boy, let's go." As he rolled over to get up, he barely spotted a shiny spec beneath a pile of leaves and slimy twigs. He crawled closer and pushed the debris away. He gasped.

Nestled beneath the pile was his mom's golden heart locket. He pinched it between his thumb and finger as if picking up a priceless jewel.

"It's the heart, boy. Maybe dad dropped it... Maybe he is still alive." He darted his head to look around. "It's only been a few weeks. Maybe he's around here somewhere, hurt."

And maybe now his mom could be normal again. She'd always believed the heart had some kind of secret power. Knowing the heart was safe might snap her out of her sadness. But if he didn't tell her he'd found it, maybe he could find the secret to the heart and it would lead him to his dad somehow. Or, maybe it could fix his foot.

It didn't matter. Right now, he had to get out of here. He gripped the heart, scooped Nick up, and raced toward home. The shadow swooped down. He tripped again, this time leaving him half-dazed. His hand hit a dead stump, loosening his fingers, and revealing the golden heart that shone in the full moonlight.

The shadow screamed like squealing pigs as it whipped the branches into a green frenzy until they blurred. Its ghoulish sounds streaked into the trees and finally faded into the depths of the forest.

The glen became eerily silent as Kristian heaved to catch his breath. He squinted at the shiny, golden heart in his palm. The heart's glow subsided in the dead, hot air, but it felt warm in his hand.

He wiped the sweat off his face. Could the heart have scared the creature?

Halfway home a light flashed across the sky. An enormous, billowy patch of luminous clouds appeared and flickered like someone flipping a light switch on and off. The clouds separated and left an ominous hole in the center. Something bright burst through the hole, leaving a glittery trail, before vanishing over the forest out of sight.

Out of nowhere, a vortex rushed through the forest, rumbling like an airplane and whipping trees in its path.

"Kristian!"

"Gracie? No, go back. Something weird's happening." It was his sister. They were twins, but the only common bond they had was their parents. And the Earth would freeze over before he'd ever admit that he didn't know what he'd do without her.

She raced toward him, despite his warnings, as the vortex sucked him and Nick into its windy tentacles. It felt as if his joints were ripping apart from his neck to his ankles, and the force sucked his dog from his arms. Kristian grunted as he stretched to grab him, but Nick twirled like a stuffed animal into the dark, windy sea.

"Kristian!" Gracie's garbled screams penetrated the crashing waves. Rain poured through the glen.

He glanced down and stared into the blood-red mouth of the shadow. As suddenly as the vortex appeared, it loosened its grip on him. He flailed as he tried to escape his fate.

TWO

Kristian's neck wrenched as his head dipped, and he landed with a thud on something soft yet firm. Before he could get his bearings, swooshing sounds washed over him, causing his skin tingle.

He had to be dead.

His vision blurred as he tried to focus. When he finally came to his senses, he saw two sets of large, milky-transparent wings. The creature swept its wings up and down in long, graceful strides. He trembled when he discovered it was a giant horse, twice the size of a Clydesdale. Its generous caramel-colored mane flowed in shiny, silk strands to thick fetlocks. Its neck was broad and muscular. The strangest thing was that its body faintly glowed and would've been invisible if not for a whisper of blue that outlined it.

"I knew it. I-I'm dead." He rubbed his neck, as fear wrapped its ugly tentacles around him. Shivers trickled down his spine.

As Gracie raced through the glen, a giant, flying, three-headed snake swooped down and plucked her up. All Kristian saw were her arms and legs flailing. Then, out of the twilight, a giant, maroon T-rex swooped in and clenched the snake's neck between its teeth. It forced its mouth open as the T-rex shook it like a rag.

Gracie dropped and floundered, but the T-rex scooped her up.

"Turn around, you beast! And save my sister!" He tugged the

horse's mane until his muscles burned, but the horse continued on its path. Kristian slid his fingers beneath the horse's hair and squeezed the base of its neck. The horse gradually made a wide turn and flew after them.

"Yes." Kristian took a deep breath. Gracie had always been a pest, but she was his sister, and he couldn't let anything happen to her. "We're coming, Gracie," he shouted.

Before the horse could reach the T-rex, it disappeared into the night with Gracie.

"No!" He kicked the horse's flanks. "Go after her."

But the great horse turned, raced toward the dark hole in the clouds, and burst into an ocean of twinkling silence. Its sheer wings became more prominent against the universe's dark backdrop, as it faintly glowed beneath the lily-white moon.

Kristian's heart thumped as he stared through space. The stars looked like silver starfish on a black beach. He brought his quivering hand to his chest, still holding the golden locket. "I'm either dreaming, or I'm dead. And if I'm not dead, I'm on my way to some heavenly realm."

He observed the black hole behind them. He couldn't understand how he could still see the meadow so vividly from this distance. Strange. Nebulae stretched like glistening towers in the distance. Their cosmic matter sparkled like colored diamond dust.

Others were bow-shaped, and some looked like tiger eyes. In the far distance, galaxies spiraled like space ships.

The horse swung his head around, and Kristian stared at its

smoky, green eyes as he held his breath and inched backward. Its hot breath spurted across his face as the big head inched its black, wet nose closer.

Kristian winced. "P-p-please…d-don't eat me. I would guess I taste t-terrible."

A sudden motion beneath him made him feel as if he was floating on a raft. The horse whinnied and smiled. Was the horse laughing at him? He wanted to chuckle when he saw the large gap between the horse's front teeth, but he covered his mouth and held it in.

The horse raised an eyebrow. "Do you really think I would eat you?"

Kristian gasped and bolted upright. "Whoa—you talk. Horses can't talk."

"Up here, yes; on Earth, no." It spoke politely with an English accent.

A bubble crept up Kristian's throat. "Am I dead?"

"No."

"Then if I'm not dead, I must be dreaming."

"No, not a dream." The horse sped off, jerking Kristian backward. "I'm sorry about your sister. I tried to rescue her."

"Well, you didn't try hard enough."

"I'm almost sure I did. And I'm almost sure that creature won't hurt her. She's a pest but not too dangerous, although she thinks she is."

"*Almost* sure she won't hurt Gracie?"

"Well, ninety-nine-point-nine percent."

Kristian shook his head. "If anything happens to her, I'm blaming you."

"Oh, really?"

"Why'd you kidnap me? Where are you taking me?"

"Well, I didn't actually kidnap you. I saved you." The horse cleared his throat as they sped through the universe. Kristian felt like his head would burst. He gritted his teeth so hard that he felt the stabbing pain in his gums. The horse cleared his throat. "Yes, I saved you. I daresay you should at least consider me a hero. If nothing else, you should be thankful. Now then, if you're coming with me, you'll need to have a bit of a better attitude, and—"

"But I didn't ask to come with you. I demand you take me home." Kristian quivered.

"Demand, huh? Do you know where you are?"

Kristian shifted his eyes everywhere. A tangerine planet and a buttery-cream moon blurred when the horse did a loop-de-loop. He clung to the horse's mane. "Stop it!"

The horse finished his loops and landed on a galactic rainbow filled with cosmic-colored particles that looked like sawdust filtering through the space.

"Wow!" Kristian swept his hand through the wet particles and got butterflies in his stomach. "Just who are you?"

"I am Sir Elliott, the great, white, blue-winged, Friesian stallion from the north." The horse curled his neck into the shape of a question mark and flicked his massive hooves with decisiveness across the rainbow as if prancing in the Queen of Scotland's Royal Guard. With great elegance and in a most distinguished manner, he stretched his front leg and bowed.

Kristian leaned backward to keep from tumbling headlong. "Sir Elliott? You're kidding, right?"

Elliott turned his head toward Kristian, who leaned back farther yet. He knew that Friesian's were great battle horses yet gentle creatures, but he didn't want to take any chances.

"So, you're from the North Pole?"

"No, I'm from the north of—"

A loud clunking noise, like a cowbell, sounded. Kristian jerked his eyes around to find the sound. "What's that noise?"

Elliott only answered with an absurd gurgle in his throat. His head shifted back and forth, and his wings twitched. He darted off the rainbow in a flash and sped through space, causing the rainbow to disappear from sight in a matter of minutes. "Hold on, lad."

"Whoa, Elliott, I'm falling." He slid down the horse's tail and dangled in slow motion.

Elliott flicked his tail, and Kristian landed back on top. The Friesian folded one set of wings around him and increased speed while the boy spit out hairs from Elliott's mane.

"What was that noise back there?"

"As I was saying, I'm from the northern country of Dia."

"What was that noise?"

"SanDorak," the horse mumbled.

"SanDorak? Was she the creature that took Gracie? If she has my sister, then why isn't Gracie screaming? Go after her." The stars turned to streams of white flashes as they raced past.

"I can't. She's gone."

"What do you mean?" Kristian swiveled his head but saw nothing. His hands shook as he slipped the remaining hair from his mouth and gripped Elliott's mane. It felt as though his heart had dropped into his stomach. "Why are you so afraid of that creature, and get all jittery whenever she's near?"

"I beg your pardon, but e-everything's under control."

Kristian sighed. He never prayed much, never really knew who to pray to, but he prayed now—to whoever was listening—that Gracie would be okay. He settled back. "So you're from Dia. Never heard of the place. What country's that in?"

"It's not a country. It's a planet."

"Sure it is. You're kidding, right?"

"No." His wings vibrated like a hummingbird's.

"What are you going to do with me?"

"Well, it's somewhat complicated."

Kristian clutched his stomach. "How so?"

"I can tell you that your destiny was set in motion when we passed through the sky portal."

"My destiny?" He gripped Elliott's mane and stood up as if he were water-skiing. He pointed a shaky finger at the horse's massive head. "What do you know about my destiny? What is my destiny, anyway? Wait a minute, you were the one who burst through those clouds and sizzled out of sight.

"Yes."

"And you act as if that was normal."

"Very. But I didn't actually sizzle."

He peered at the back of Elliott's head. *Just maybe…* "Can you make noises like a screaming monkey?"

"I'm shocked that you would ask that. I should think you'd be a little more grateful than to call me a monkey. I assure you I cannot make monkey noises. What are monkeys?"

Kristian shook his head, wiped his face, and lowered his head. "Never mind. Besides, I didn't *call* you a monkey. I asked if you could scream like one. The day my dad disappeared, I heard monkey screams. Did you take my dad?"

"I'm sorry for your father's misfortune, but I assure you, I did not—"

"Well, you took me didn't you?"

"But I did not take your father. And I'm sorry to say, it wouldn't be wise to take you home. Going back through that portal could mean changing your destiny, and you may not like the outcome."

"What is my destiny?"

"I'm not at liberty to say. Quite frankly, I'm not sure."

"This is just great." Kristian fell backward and bumped his head on Elliott's bulging muscles. He slipped the family photo from the back pocket of his jeans and ran his thumb across his dad's face. He'd carried it with him since his dad's disappearance.

"I guess I could go against my instincts, but if I take you back, I can't accept the responsibility of a bad result. Your choice. Do you wish to go back, or be safe?"

"Some choice." Kristian groaned. "I'm utterly... completely...doomed."

The horse zipped through the cosmos, and Kristian tightened his muscles when he noticed an obscure light waving in the distance, like a thin sheet in a tender breeze. It kept pace with them, and then it vanished.

THREE

Another Friesian, this one pecan-colored, swooped in beside Elliott. Its dark lashes intensified sapphire eyes. A shiny, ivory mane flowed to its fetlocks, but unlike Elliott, its wings were a whisper of cream. Its steps were high as the horse flew, and its movements were so effortless that it calmed Kristian's nerves.

"It's about time. I wondered what was taking you so long, bro." The voice was tender and ladylike. "I thought you might need my help. I know how you and—"

"Pa-leeze. And how many times must I tell you to stop calling me bro?" Elliott shook his head. "Kristian, this is Sabrina." He snorted, and Kristian caught the tail end of the snort. A smack of slobber splattered on his cheek, and he wiped the slimy film away. "Now, fly away."

"Nice to meet you, Kristian. I'll see you boys inside." Sabrina grinned. One of her front teeth was a bit longer than the other tooth. She zoomed off and squirted a trail of what appeared to be stardust in Elliott's face.

"Show off." Elliott spit and sputtered.

Kristian giggled. "Inside?" He liked her. She reminded him a bit of— He thought about Gracie and hoped she was okay.

"You are about to see where I live. Sabrina watches over

Dia's southern portion, as I said, and Drake, who has a lovely family, watches over the east. I watch the north. We're Dia's gatekeepers."

Kristian's mouth slipped open as they soared toward a monstrous, hollow, black orb.

"Ahhh, what a comforting sight. This, lad, is Dia's Life Gate, entrance to the kingdom." It sounded as if Elliott had slipped into a daydream; his voice was airy and surreal. It felt as though they were entering a land of enchantment. Kristian stared at the dazzling, blue ring around the orb. The orb looked like a wormhole. He'd studied wormholes in Mr. Karr's seventh grade science class, but he had always been skeptical of their existence and doubted whether they were short paths that linked one place to another.

As they drew nearer, his stomach felt like he had just topped the first dip of a roller coaster. At the entrance, there were two colossal, angelic figures, one on each side, wearing a white flowing gown. Each one had an arm arched over their head and their forefinger touching the other's. They smiled gently as Elliott drifted past golden gates that opened just before they reached the entrance. One of the figures winked at Kristian, which caused his heart to flutter. Above the orb's entrance, he noticed the same obscure light that he had seen moments ago waving in the distance.

Elliott drifted through the swirling mist. "Dia means *to guard*. The Kingdom of Dia has been a safe haven for many weary souls. It is the gateway to the northern Trifold Galaxies. No one can get to them unless they pass through Dia."

A tick of excitement pinched Kristian's skin and replaced some of his fears. Bubbles popped against his face as Elliott glided through the hourglass center, and he chuckled when Elliott's lips jiggled in the breeze.

They glided through the wormhole until they reached the end and entered what Kristian thought was going to be an enchanted land. But instead, the land didn't have one drop of enchantment, and was as far from a Garden of Eden as anyone could imagine. The planet looked like it was dying from the middle outward.

"What's going on? It looks like the only thing living is that oak tree."

"I'm afraid death is pushing its tentacles around our planet." Elliott flew up the side of Dia's highest mountain. Kristian got a weird feeling. The place looked so familiar—

But that was totally impossible.

"Oh, no." Elliott stared at Kristian. "Your hands…and your face."

"What about th—" He lifted his hands. They glowed faintly and then faded. "What's up with that?"

Elliott narrowed his eyes. "Very strange, indeed."

"How come you aren't glowing as bright as you were outside of Dia?"

The Friesian tried to explain. "Dians have a gene that reacts to different wavelengths of light. The gene controls the intensity of our glow. Sometimes we glow brighter than other times. It's like your DNA—everyone is different. Light is our greatest source of strength. Without it, we grow weak and eventually die." He sighed. "Lately, the gene seems to be growing weaker because Dia's light is fading."

"Why's your voice sounding all weird—like there are two of you speaking?" He wrinkled his nose.

"This is how we sound on Dia, but I'm curious to know why your voice sounds so strange, like you're a tad hoarse."

Kristian cleared his throat. "Probably catching a cold."

"A cold?"

"Never mind." He shook his head. A pungent odor lingered through the air. "What's that smell?"

"Decay, I would assume. Strange events have been happening since King Aaron disappeared."

"King Aaron? You mean real king lives here?" Kristian's heart quivered. "What happened to him?"

"No one knows. He just disappeared one day, and the Dians haven't been the same since. They depended on him for everything. They've become stoic…like, unemotional robots, I guess."

Kristian thought about how dependent he was on Gracie. He could relate. If anything had happened to her, he'd probably become stoic, too.

"Do you still have your mother's golden heart?"

He swallowed hard as he stared at the back of the big horse's head. "H-How'd you know about that?"

Elliott sighed. "I must tell you, I don't believe you are here by chance. This place holds your destiny."

"What makes you say that?"

The Friesian remained silent. Birds cawed and swooped around them as they climbed higher up the mountainside. A wavy barrier surrounded the planet, and beyond the barrier, a bright light shone in the far distance, like the light he and his dad had spotted through his telescope on clear nights.

A clear, cascading waterfall streamed over several plateaus before plunging into a lake of frothy foam. Copper-topped roofs dotted the valley of cottages on tiny islets with a wooden bridge that connected each cottage to land. He shivered when he spotted a dark forest in the west. It looked just like the one back home.

Pushing the thought of the forest aside, he pretended for a moment he was visiting one of his princely friends until he remembered that he had no friends—only Gracie. When Elliott cleared the mountaintop, Kristian thought his heart would burst at the sight of a majestic, sandstone castle, but it looked dull with dead ivy vines that seemed as if they had dried up and stopped climbing months ago.

"This…is Mighty Loft." Elliott dashed through a faded rainbow arched over the castle and headed for the stables, where eager black stallions poked their nodding heads through olive green stall doors and whinnied as he flew overhead.

After circling the stables, they headed back toward the castle. As they descended toward the octagon, brick courtyard that glistened like sugar cookies, a cowbell clunked again. Elliott flicked and flailed like a baby bird floundering from its nest.

Kristian lurched and dangled from his tail. "Elliott!"

"Oh, I was hoping this would be—" He grunted and snorted. His hindquarters and wings jerked at the same time. Then everything went haywire. His wings twitched. They twittered. They twerked. "I wanted so much to impress you…with a graceful…descent."

"Well, so much for that plan." Kristian's fingers ached as he slid through Elliott's tail.

"Somebody help me right now!"

Kristian didn't have to peer through the foggy clouds to know whose voice that was. "Gracie!" He saw the huge outline of the creature that was carrying her—SanDorak.

"Get me down! This beast is going to kill me!"

Kristian thought she might blow her lungs out. "Get Gracie, Elliott." His hands slipped through Elliott's tail, trapping his foot in his hairs. Blood rushed to his head as he dangled upside down, jerking his head around trying to keep his sister in sight.

Elliott jolted. "SanDorak, let go of her."

Kristian thought his head would burst. He glanced down and noticed a group of kids huddled in the courtyard near the fountain. "Get me down."

"Do not fear…everything is under control," Elliott wheezed. "Al…most…down."

"You're soaking wet," Kristian shouted, "and you're dripping on me."

Elliott gasped. "Sorry."

"You sure have everything under control all right."

"Where's Sabrina when I need her?"

"You told her to get lost, remember?"

"Yes, well—"

SanDorak growled and shot a stream of fire, missing them by inches. The tips of her ragged wings looked like they got caught in a blender. The gray clouds swirled around her, making her ruby eyes appear like red lasers.

Kristian began hyperventilating; his heart raced, and he felt like he was suffocating when the same clunking noise sounded.

"Get me off this beast," Gracie hollered. "It looks like something out of the pages of one of your harebrained fantasy books."

Kristian's head spun. From what he could see, what kept her from falling was a long strand of the creature's sparse hair wrapped around her arm. SanDorak shook her head and flung green slime through the air, slapping his head. The potent, moldy-cheese smell stung his eyes.

SanDorak rammed Elliott in his side, and Gracie lost her grip. Elliott floundered and managed to thrust his wing out and catch her before she hit the ground, but at the same time, it caused Kristian to drop from his tail, plunging him to the ground.

He rolled down a hill and halted beneath a bush, where he clutched his throbbing shoulder and winced. Swooshing sounds passed above the bush and stopped.

The breeze smelled like fresh air. He peeked through the limbs and caught the glimpse of a faint light. When he struggled from beneath the bush, his head jerked back as if someone had stepped on his hair.

"Ouch! Elliott, stop messing around. Get off my hair."
He tugged, but he couldn't break free.

"Kristian MacNeal," said a soft, wispy voice. "Your journey

has now begun."

He tightened his burning muscles and held his breath. It was definitely not Elliott.

FOUR

Kristian squinted through the rustling leaves. "Who are you?"

A faint light glowed beneath a thin, shimmering veil. Whatever it was had no flesh and bones. He gripped the back of his hair again and tugged, but it wouldn't release him.

"You have been born for this moment in time." The voice sounded like a soft whisper in his ear.

"Who are you?" He squinted, annoyed with his dilemma.

The light floated and danced up and down in small movements. "The Kingdom of Dia is in grave danger. It will become extinct if you do not find the key to the golden heart locket and destroy the shadowy creature that roams this forest."

Kristian cringed. Golden heart locket? Shadowy creature? Had the creature followed him here?

"Your destiny was set in motion when you took your mother's ancient, golden heart locket. Her destiny has become yours, and now you must fulfill it."

"How do you know that I—what are you? How do you know my mom? How do you know about the heart?" He tried jerking his head again. "Ouch! Let go."

"Listen to me."

He froze. He could barely breathe because of his nerves. Where was Gracie when he needed her?

"The key to the golden heart will unlock the secret that you will need to fulfill your obligation."

"But—ouch—obligation?"

"Hold tight to the heart. Guard it with your life, and listen to my still, small voice along the way."

"Oh, brother. I don't think so. Why do I— How can I— What makes you think I can fulfill my mom's destiny? I don't even know what her destiny is."

"Right now, Dia's future is uncertain. The white book will show you where to begin; it will guide you. Then it is up to you to follow the right path." The voice faded with the image.

"Wait." Kristian scrambled from beneath the bush and hobbled down the path. He bent over to catch his breath. "What key? What white book? Come back."

Gracie tramped down the path toward him brushing herself off. "What happened to you? I fell a gazillion feet, and if it hadn't been for that horse of yours, I'd be a goner."

"He's not my horse. And where were you when I needed you?" He was glad SanDorak hadn't eaten her, but she always found a way to get on his last nerve. "Something pinned me to the ground and—"

She peered at him. "Who were you talking to?"

"Did you see some weird light float past you?"

"You fell on your head too hard." She sighed. "You look a little weird. Your eyes are hazy, and—"

"I don't look weird." Kristian glanced around. "It spoke to

me."

Gracie shook her head. "What spoke to you?"

"The light."

"Okay, what'd it say?"

He told her everything except for the part that he had their mom's golden heart locket.

"You, fulfill Mom's destiny?" She snickered. "How does that, whatever that thing was, even know Mom, anyway? And what destiny?" She glanced around and wrinkled her nose. "Where are we? I must have passed out on that beast because I don't remember anything. We can't be too far from home."

"I hate to be the one to break this to you, but... we're on another planet in another galaxy."

"Stop teasing." She giggled. "Why aren't you laughing?"

Kristian told her everything he knew.

"Tell me you're making this up just to get back at me for something."

"I'm telling the truth."

"Well, how are we going to get home?" Her voice raised an octave. "What are we going to do?"

"How do I know?"

"You don't have to be so snippety." She slapped her hands on her hips and glared at him. "What else did this veiled light say?"

"I'm supposed to find a white book." Kristian rubbed his tingly scalp and walked off. She caught up to him. Her freckles had already turned a darker shade of red, which meant she was perturbed.

Sabrina tried to untangle Elliott's mane from a bush. A blond girl swayed with her hands behind her back, staring at them from across the courtyard.

"Who's that?" Gracie asked. "Let's go make friends with her."

"Wait—" Kristian grabbed her arm, but she shook his grip and strolled toward the girl, swinging her arms. But the girl rushed away and disappeared inside the castle.

A ruckus of chirping and twittering broke out in what looked like a blueberry orchard down the hill. A flock of bluebirds carried on as if they were trying to get attention on purpose. He hobbled down the path to check it out.

That's when he noticed the oversized blueberries hanging on branches like deep blue cotton balls and ready to burst. His mouth watered. He had discovered blueberry heaven.

But when he took a closer look, he noticed fading leaves jiggling. He tiptoed closer and heard chomping, slurping, and gulping. He bent down to investigate and spotted a black, wet nose sticking through a small gap between the branches.

"Hello?" said a strange, stuffy voice. The creature spoke slowly with a drawl, punctuated with sniffs and snorts. "Could you please help?"

He peered closer. "What's wrong?"

"My nose…it's stuck. It feels numb, and my tail… Well, I'm afraid I lost sight of my tail. Can you see it?"

Kristian followed the long, busy tail wrapped around another bush.

"Oh, dear, my heart's racing. I can barely breathe. I think I'm dying," the creature said.

"You're probably just hyperventilating." Kristian shook his head.

"Hyper-what-alating?"

"Hyperventilating is too much excitement caused by a dramatic event. It causes your heart to race, and you think you're having a heart attack."

"Sounds dangerous. Do hurry and get me out of here."

"It's not dangerous." He tried to calm the little creature as he unwrapped its tail from the bush and dragged it across the ground. He spread the branches of the bush from around the creature's nose, but he lost his grip, and the branches snapped back.

"Ouch!"

"Ooooh, sorry." He pried the branches apart but again lost his grip.

The animal snorted. "I can clearly see that this is not working. Please, summon help. I've lost all feeling in my nose now. Is it swelling?"

Kristian could barely make out what the creature was saying between the wheezing, sneezing, and spraying saliva in his face.

"Hold still, will you?" He wiped his face and pried the branches apart again. "Hurry, get out."

The little creature jiggled until he finally squirmed free, landing on his rump. "Whew! I was eating those berries and got stuck. I thought the bushes would devour me."

Kristian wanted to laugh as he stared into a miniature donkey's deep green eyes. His long, furry ears touched the ground. He was a little hairier than most donkeys and no taller than Kristian's thighs. Finally, he couldn't hold it in and laughed. "I don't mean to laugh, but you do look—"

"Aw, it's okay." The donkey sighed. His ears slid across the ground as he waddled farther down the hill. "I'm used to it—runt of the family, you know. I'm Sirus."

Kristian hobbled to catch up. Sabrina was still trying to untangle Elliott's tail from the bush.

"I knew he wouldn't be much help." Sirus nodded toward Elliott. "He is forever in some kind of a predicament. He's clumsy, he is. Do you like blueberries?" A purple dribble slid down the side of the donkey's mouth.

"They're my favorite."

"When I eat blueberries, my eyes sometimes turn glassy, and I can momentarily forget where I am."

"I thought I had it bad." Kristian chuckled. "How do you manage to get through life with such a long tail and ears?"

Sirus's purple teeth showed through his thin grin. "I can get into a bit of trouble now and again but, so far, nothing too serious. We should laugh at ourselves sometimes, don't you think?"

Kristian glanced at his foot and frowned.

"Oh, dear, I am sorry, so sorry. I didn't notice—"

"How could you *not* notice?"

They meandered toward a large pond near the base of a hill

next to a large rock garden and sat down. Faded pink and blue flowers poked their heads between the rocks.

"I hate it." Kristian stared at a violet-flowered lily pad floating near the pond's edge. A frog croaked and jumped to another lily pad.

"I can tell, but—" Sirus dropped to the ground in a flash as if someone had kicked his stubby legs out from under him. He rolled and twisted and flicked his legs. Red splotches spread across his thick, tan belly.

"What's wrong? Are you dying this time?" Kristian grunted as he tried to roll the donkey over, but he was heavier than he looked.

"Hurry." Sirus shouted, twisting and wriggling.

"Hurry and do what?"

"Scratch me all over, head to toe—quick." Sirus bucked and squirmed. One of his hooves whizzed past Kristian's ear. "The blueberries, I'm allergic to them."

"Stop kicking, will you?" He formed his hands into claws and scratched his new friend's tough hide from top to bottom.

"Ah, ooh, yes, don't stop."

"You shouldn't be eating blueberries if you're allergic to them."

"I can't help it…I'm hooked."

"I'm sorry, but I can't feel one bit sorry for you now." He slapped a hand on his forehead and hobbled off.

"Wait; it's not my fault." Sirus scrambled to his hooves and padded across the brick path.

Kristian shook his head and kept going. He didn't stop until he reached the crystal-clear river that swept through Dia's sprawling valley. He sat on the stiff grass, plucked some tan blades, and tossed them in the breeze. Sirus wiggled his rump on the ground, sprawled his hind legs, and rested his front hooves between them. He gazed at the river. Kristian could see the donkey out of the corner of his eye, staring at him.

"When I was on Earth," Sirus began, turning his gaze to the river, "I —"

"Wait a minute." Kristian shifted his weight. "You mean you're from Earth?"

"I've been there a few times, yes."

His heart quivered. He felt instantly connected to Sirus. He tapped his finger on his chest. "My sister and I are from Earth. How'd you end up here?"

"It's too long of a story. How about you?"

He decided to tell Sirus everything. He couldn't explain why he liked this little animal right off, unless it was because he felt like he could trust him, as if he had finally found a true friend. The words poured out like a waterfall—about his foot, his dad, Alon, and even the golden heart and the key.

"But please," he begged, "you can't tell anyone about the heart. Not even my sister."

Sirus nodded. "Your secret's safe. As I recall, there's a legend that surrounds Alon."

Kristian's eyes widened. "You mean you know about Alon?" His voice shrieked. "Tell me, what legend?"

"Allegedly, a king and his knights ran into an ambush one night. They raced their horses through the forest, and it's been told that they vanished through a tree without a trace. Some say they disappeared into thin air; others say they disappeared into Alon. But the strangest thing, legend has it that they came from the Caledonian Forest near Perth, Scotland."

Kristian sat in stunned silence for a few seconds. "The tree does have a giant opening and…" he stared, and his mouth slowly dropped open. His mind swirled with thoughts of a particular king that he had been intrigued with for a long while. "What do you think happened?"

"Well, legend claims the tree's opening is a," he leaned closer and whispered, "a portal."

Kristian blinked. Then his face froze for a few seconds as if he'd seen a monster. He finally found his voice. "There's a creature not made of flesh and bones that lives in that forest." He bit his bottom lip, hoping to get some secret information about the shadow. Sirus gazed at the river as if his mind had wandered to another place in time.

"Whenever I got too close to it, branches swayed as if they were trying to warn me to stay away. Do you think that tree could've swallowed my Dad?"

Sirus gazed at him. "Do you?"

He slipped the golden heart from his pocket and unfolded his fingers. It felt warm in his palm. "I'd give anything to know this heart's secret. My mom said the heart holds some kind of power. I've been secretly hoping that it might have the power to fix my foot, and well,

I've never told anyone this before, but…I wish I could travel so far back in time to a place where my foot could be normal. Do you think time travel is possible?"

The little creature sat silent before responding. "I do. When I saw you earlier, you had fallen off Elliott and rolled beneath a bush. It looked like something was standing on your hair preventing you from getting up. You were speaking to it. May I ask who it was?"

Kristian looked around to make sure no one was listening. "It was some kind of light covered by a dusky veil."

Sirus's eyes bulged. He froze as if he went into a trance.

FIVE

"Hello?" Kristian waved his hand in front of Sirus's face. "Snap out of it."

When Sirus finally came to his senses, he paced. "Oh my, this is most significant, most significant indeed. I— Not everyone sees it."

"What are you talking about? Not everyone sees what?"

"Tell me exactly what happened." His eyes by now were well rounded.

Kristian told him. When he finished, Sirus sat. "The veiled light only seeks those who are searching for something. What are you seeking?"

"I told you; I'm seeking the secret of the golden heart and the key that unlocks it."

He shook his head vigorously. "No, it has to be something that you can't see or touch."

"I don't have a clue then." Kristian bit his fingernail and spit it out.

"The veiled light is not flesh and bone. That's why it's only concerned with someone who isn't seeking material things. When it found me, I was quite confounded."

"You mean you've seen it?" Kristian jumped to his feet and put his hands on his hips. Sirus nodded. "Why did it seek you?"

"To prepare me."

"For what?"

"I'm not at liberty... I cannot say."

"Well, whatever it is, I don't have time to be bothered by it. I need to find the key to the heart."

"Tsk, tsk, tsk." Sirus shook his head. "Do not think you can hide from the veiled light, and you'd be unwise to ignore it."

"You don't know me very well." Kristian fumbled with the small mole below his left ear as he always did when he was afraid. "When someone tells me to do or not to do something, I usually do the opposite."

The donkey stuck his nose in the air and harrumphed. "I see you have much to learn before you discover your true mission and what you are truly searching for."

He scrunched his nose. "How would you know, anyway?"

"Faith." Sirus said as he waddled off. "Faith believes in someone or something, even when you can't see or touch them or it."

"Whatever that means." Kristian kicked a loose rock and it skittered across the path. "I don't know anything about faith. The extent of my faith is that my sister gets on my nerves. And I don't have to see that to believe it." He looked at his foot. "And, if I don't find the key or the secret to this heart, I may never fix my foot or find my dad."

Sirus sighed. "Physical things aren't as important as what goes on inside your heart. Faith begins in the heart, and it believes in something bigger than you, even when things don't make sense."

After a long silence, Kristian said, "Well, I think the veiled light got ahold of the wrong person with me."

"The light never gets the wrong person," said a soft voice.

Kristian flinched and turned his head. It was the same blond girl he and Gracie had seen earlier.

"That light is *your* light." She was tall and slender and wore two white lilies on the side of her waist-length, wavy hair. Kristian figured she was the same age as him but slightly taller. She also had a faint glow about her like Elliott and the others.

"My dear, Linnea," Sirus said, "how have you been?"

"Fine, thanks." Her smile revealed dimples. Her white, silk pants—something like you'd see on a genie—blew in the breeze. "I didn't think I'd see you so soon."

"I was summoned." The donkey smiled.

"What do you mean you were summoned?" Kristian glanced at him. "From where?"

"I didn't mean to eavesdrop." Linnea smiled at Kristian. "But don't get it in your head that you'll be able to shake that veiled light because you won't. And you won't be able to hide from it either, so don't get any ideas."

Sirus shuffled off. Linnea limped after him, her rose scent lingering in the air.

"Hey, do you guys know anything about a white book?" he called out, but they had disappeared through a grove of pines. When he glanced up at the wormhole, it had shrunk since he'd arrived on Dia. But the light outside of Dia in the east shined bright through the clouds. The cool air brushed across his face.

***

Back at the castle, Kristian stopped in front of a black wrought-iron fence surrounding the courtyard. Frogs croaked their chorus songs. Willow branches cast thin shadows across the moat as their tips brushed across the top. But he hadn't seen any adult Dians.

Gracie shuffled up behind him. "Mom's probably frantic by now. Can't we just go home?"

"Elliott said Earth isn't safe right now."

"Why not?"

The wet scent of hay drifted through the air as hooves clicked across the courtyard.

"Ah, Sirus, I'm glad to see you again." Sabrina bent down and kissed the top of Sirus's head.

He smiled. "And you as well."

Elliott stumbled, bumped into Sabrina, and glared at Sirus, who cleared his throat and nodded in acknowledgment.

The stallion lowered his nose and snorted in the little donkey's face. "Do tell, what brings you here this time to annoy us?"

"Nothing that concerns you. Now, back away, you're breath—"

Elliott swung his head and pressed his velvety nose against Kristian's ear. "I'm sorry you fell off of me. I didn't mean for that to happen. My wings can go all haywire sometimes. Are you okay?"

Kristian nodded. "I'm fine."

"Seems to happen whenever SanDorak shows up." Sirus smirked.

Elliott nudged his nose into Sirus's face, lip quivering. "That's utter nonsense." He turned to Kristian. "By the way, who were you speaking with? It looked as if something had your head pinned to the ground, but I saw no one."

The boy squinted at Sirus, hoping he would keep quiet. The group of kids giggled. His face turned warm when he remembered the first day of seventh grade when he'd overheard a group of kids snicker about his foot.

Elliott nibbled Kristian's hair. "Ouch, what are you doing?"

"Pretty sure they're laughing at these." He tugged two small twigs from his hair and dropped them on the ground. "They sort of looked like a deer's antlers."

Gracie shook her head and giggled. He gave his sister *the look*—a cold, unblinking stare, furrowed eyebrows—and studied the kids standing across the way. One was missing an arm, another kid was bald, and another had a foot missing. Kristian swallowed hard; at least he had two feet.

Elliott nodded to the kids. "They accept their flaws because they know that life isn't always fair. They know that what's in their hearts—love, kindness, patience—is more important than what they look like on the outside."

Kristian thought about what Elliott said as he hobbled across the sandstone bridge to the diamond-shaped inner courtyard in front of the castle. The dry ivy vines sprawled across parts of the castle walls caused them to look like a maze. He stopped, and Gracie bumped into him, almost knocking him down.

"I have a weird feeling about this place," she whispered. "I don't think I'd go in there if I were you."

He stared at her but crept up the steps to the portico anyway. The massive emerald doors loomed above him. She sighed. He tightened his fingers around his thumbs as he bent his head and looked straight up. Low-hanging clouds drifted across the castle's turrets.

"Before you go in, follow me." Sirus waddled behind the castle and down some stairs. Kristian followed him to a stuffy room below the castle. A candle flickered, casting a warbled light across the mosaic floor made of greens, blues, dark browns, and tans. A scuffed and dented armored suit stood atop a bronze dais. He slid his fingers across the suit's pauldrons then the spaulders and vambraces and finally to the gauntlets. His heart fluttered.

"Destiny brought you here." Sirus's eyes glinted in the candlelight.

"What are you talking about?" He crept around the suite, sliding his fingers across the cool metal.

Sirus flicked his hoof against the base of the dais. A drawer opened. He lifted a scroll with his teeth. "Helf me pleaf."

Kristian stepped on one end of the scroll while Sirus unrolled it with his nose. The scribbles written on the scroll looked medieval.

"This scroll is part of your destiny now. The veiled light called me back here. I am to show you this scroll, where wisdom has left its mark."

A warm breeze embraced Kristian like an invisible cloak. He widened his eyes, eager to know what the scroll said.

Sirus began reading.

"Our enemies come to steal, kill, and destroy. They go to great measures to tempt us into believing that right is wrong and wrong is right. They want us to doubt the truth." He glanced at the helmet of the armor. "First they try to penetrate our helmets to destroy our minds because knowledge frightens them. Therefore, we must protect our minds at all costs."

The donkey glanced at the breastplate and continued. "The breastplate protects one's heart, a most vital organ. It's easy to believe lies if we don't have a firm foundation of the truth. Our greatest battle is the war waged against our minds and hearts, and we must guard them at all times—you must turn from trouble whenever possible."

"But that's being a coward."

"It's being smart." Sirus pulled a pair of brown leather, knee-high boots from the drawer. "Put these on."

"Those look ridiculous."

"They will remind you that there will be times when you must flee your enemies and other times when you must stand firm and face your fears, fight for what is right. But beware; you must choose your battles wisely and allow wisdom to guide you."

Kristian tried to understand all of it. "But how am I supposed to know the difference? I'm just a kid."

"You must listen and watch, and you will figure it out."

"Why are you telling me these things?" He grunted as he slipped on the boots. He put his hands on his hips. "I just want to find the key and the secret to the golden heart and leave this place. I don't want to fight anyone."

Sirus handed him a piece of parchment paper from the drawer and sighed. "Please, read."

Kristian unrolled the paper and began to read. "For I know the plans I have for you, plans to prosper you, and not to harm you, plans to give you hope and a future." He flicked his eyes at Sirus. "Who wrote this?"

"Turn it over."

The paper scrunched in his hands.

"My dear Sirus," Kristian read aloud, "someone is coming to save Dia. You will know him when you meet him. Help the lad along—Dia is in grave danger." A slimy glob stuck in the middle of his throat. The paper slipped from his fingers and drifted to the floor.

Sirus waddled across the room and nudged a wooden door open with his nose. Kristian peered into the small room.

"A sword? What do you expect me to do with that?" He slid his fingers lightly down the blade and lifted it. The sword weighed no more than a bottle of water. A warm feeling swept over him as he eyed the hilt's intricate design. The pommel was emerald green, heart-shaped, and trimmed in gold. Below the heart was a pair of eagle claws clutching several fig leaves. The handle was apple red. Engraved in the top portion of the shiny blade was the word *Cased.* "What does that mean?"

"His love endures forever."

"Whose love?"

"The one who has plans for you, the one who knows your future. In other words, the one who knows best."

Kristian shook his head and slid the tip of his finger across his mole. "How could anyone know my future? I'm really not interested in sword fighting. Gracie's the hunter in the family, not me. I'd rather sit down with a good book and dream about kingdoms and unknown creatures. I've never hurt anybody or anything in my life."

"Suit yourself. I hope you won't have to use it." Sirus turned and waddled away.

"Where we going?" He clasped both hands around the sword's handle and swiped the blade through the air, then lurched forward and accidentally scraped the sword against the wall, the floor, and finally across the low ceiling.

Sirus dove to the floor. The sword just missed his head by a cat's whisker. He slid on his stomach and bumped into the wall. "Easy with that."

Something strange came over Kristian. The sword felt good in his hands, almost natural. He felt brave. He pivoted, lost his balance, and dropped on the floor. The sword clanked and slid.

The little donkey jumped up on all fours, scrambled in the opposite direction, and shivered like a cold, wet dog. "I do hope you get the hang of that before innocent beings get hurt."

"Sorry. It got away from me. You okay?" Kristian gasped as he struggled to his feet, rubbed his sweaty hands on his pants, and lifted the sword. "I warned you. I'm not going to use this thing. And besides, what good is a sword if a person can't control it?"

"Well, it just might be the person using it. You'll get the hang of it," Sirus mumbled, as he strode out the door and up the steps. "I hope." He cleared his throat. "Are you ready to meet the king now?"

"I thought the king was missing?" He tugged the sheath around his hips and slid the sword down.

"That was King Aaron. I'm talking about King Malakon."

SIX

The tip of the sword scratched each step as Kristian followed Sirus to the courtyard.

"King Malakon is King Ramón's son, from the Planet Lia." He nodded in the direction of the bright light shining in the east. "He made himself King of Dia when King Aaron disappeared. He is sly, and the Dians are afraid of him. They try to stay hidden."

So that's why he hadn't seen many Dians. Kristian stood in front of the emerald-green castle doors. One flung open, causing him to shuffle backward and step on top of Gracie's foot.

"Ouch!" She shoved him forward with her fingertips.

"Well, stop sneaking up on me."

A tall, slender man stepped out from behind the door. The man wore a green, tri-folded cap that reminded Kristian of William Tell, the guy who'd shot an apple off his son's head. His light brown hair swept across his forehead. He wanted to chuckle but didn't. The only thing missing was a white feather sticking from the cap.

Gracie tapped the back of Kristian's leg with her foot and mumbled. He nudged her with his elbow.

The man fumbled with a silver skeleton key hanging from a thin rope around his waist. He wore a white shirt that hung to the middle of his thighs over royal blue tights and black, knee-high boots.

He was handsome, tall, and thin but intimidating.

A short man peeked around the man's waist. He wore a brown robe like a monk's, and he had a thick, crimson rope hugging his waist. An oversized hood hung over the man's tan, wrinkled forehead, stopping just above his bushy, dark gray brows. Wisps of gray hair curled around the sides of his face.

"Who are you?" the slender man asked as he groped his chin and furrowed his brows.

"K-Kristian MacNeal."

"Let him in, Mikal, and stop acting like a hot shot." Linnea strolled in.

Mikal sighed, and his face turned a tinted rose color, obviously embarrassed.

Sirus nodded. "Go on, step aside."

The slender man lowered his head and stepped aside. Kristian accidentally stepped on his foot as he passed. Mikal grunted and backed into the stubby man.

"Out of my way, Gerwin."

Gerwin? That name sounded familiar.

Gerwin hustled down the hall and out of sight. Kristian glanced at Linnea, who shrugged and wandered off across the courtyard.

"Who are you?" Kristian asked Mikal.

He bowed his head. "The king's most trusted servant."

Sirus mumbled the same words at the same time.

Gracie tripped through the doorway and rammed into Kristian, almost knocking him to the floor. Mikal grabbed her arm and stood her back on her feet before she plopped on top of Kristian.

"You have to stay here while I take Kristian in to see the king," Mikal told her.

She snapped her arm back. "I go with my brother."

Kristian shook his head and scanned the large octagon foyer. The top half of the walls had angelic paintings, while white stone covered the bottom half. The floor looked like onyx. Sirus tapped Kristian's shin with his hoof.

"Ouch." He rubbed it up and down. "What?"

The donkey nodded. Across the room stood a black stone pedestal. On top—

"The white book," Kristian gasped. His foot ached as he limped toward it.

"Leave that alone," Mikal said, but Kristian ignored him.

The cover was white velvet with white pages trimmed in gold. His fingers quivered as he reached to open the book, but Mikal seized his wrist.

"Follow me."

He jerked his wrist away.

Elliott stumbled through the doorway and clopped across the floor as he struggled to get his balance. After composing himself, he said, "Mikal, leave him alone."

Kristian opened the book and stared at the picture on the first page—a man on a white horse.

"You?" He glanced at Elliott, who nodded.

The man in the book wore a white robe. In his left hand, he

held a sword just like the one Kristian had carried from the room below the castle. There was a thick, white book tucked beneath the man's arm and a mole beneath his left ear.

By now, Kristian's goosebumps had goosebumps. He stared at Sirus as Gracie's hot breath spurted across the back of his neck. He gestured for her to get back. Instead, she peeked farther over his shoulder.

"Why would anybody set a wordless book on such a lovely pedestal?"

He turned and stared at her. "You mean you don't see anything on this page?"

She shrugged. "No."

Elliott cleared his throat and nudged his nose between them to whisper, "This is your life book. Whenever someone new arrives on Dia, a new book arrives. You're the only one who can see these pages." He peered at Sirus. "Well, you and you-know-who here."

"If that's true then Gracie should have a book." Kristian glanced around.

"Clearly, hers hasn't arrived yet," Sirus said.

"Why not?" She put her hands on her waist. "Mine should be here too."

Kristian peered at her. "You're not even supposed to be here. That's why you don't have one. This is my journey, not yours." He didn't dare tell her he was glad she was here.

"Then why am I here? I have to have a book somewhere." She crossed her arms and flicked her eyes between Sirus and Elliott.

Sirus snorted. "Gracie, please, calm down."

Kristian glanced at the book and remembered the veiled light's words: *You were born for this moment in time.* If that were true, then Gracie would've had to be born for this moment in time too, because they were twins. She had to have a book around here somewhere. Could it be her journey too, and he didn't know it?

He studied Mikal. "Tell me why I'm here."

"Yeah, why are *we* here?" Gracie pursed her lips.

Mikal rubbed his jaw and leered at them all. "King Malakon believes that Dia is in danger. And for some unknown reason," he glanced at Kristian, "he thinks you can save it."

"Me? That's crazy."

Gracie lifted her hand to her mouth and smirked. "Yeah, right."

"He doesn't even know me." Kristian flipped to the next page. "Why would he—"

He drew in a breath when the past events of his life sprang into action across the pages, fading in and out from one event to another like a movie. In one scene, he threw a pacifier across the room. Gracie climbed out of her crib, rescued it, tottered back, and tossed it over the railing.

In another scene, he fell off his bike. His sister eagerly helped him up, put his feet on the pedals, and wobbled down the sidewalk beside him.

In another scene, they looked for Nick all night in the pouring rain.

It was the last scene that his heart almost leaped within him.

When he ran out of the house this morning, who followed him? As always, it was Gracie.

He turned the page and saw a picture of a castle. Growing beside the castle was a mustard tree that looked just like the one his dad had given him when he was young. His dad had told him the tree's seeds were like grains of sand, and yet they were still able to grow into a tree fifteen feet or higher.

Kristian's temples thumped. He pushed past Gracie, rushed out the door, and didn't stop until he was out of breath.
He bent over and gripped his knees.

Gracie rushed up. "What'd you see in that book?"

"Nothing. Leave me alone." He squinted. Gracie's freckles darkened. She was perturbed.

"Well, something happened. Why'd you run out of there?"

He wanted to confide in her, to tell her he had their mom's golden heart, but he didn't know if she could keep the secret even if she pinky-swore, which she didn't like doing. 'My word is my word,' she always said. If she knew he had the heart, she'd go ballistic.

"Can't a guy have any secrets?"

"You have secrets? What secrets? I won't tell. I promise. I pinky—never mind. I won't tell."

SEVEN

A small, blue flash whizzed past Gracie's face. She snapped her head back. When it whizzed past Kristian, he jerked his head and thumped it on his sister's forehead.

"Ouch!" She rubbed the spot and nudged away from him. The blue flash whizzed around. "What is that thing?"

Kristian ducked. It grazed the tip of his nose, stinging him like a paper cut. "Ouch! How do I know? Maybe it's a weird looking Dian bee."

He stared so intensely that his head whirled for a second. The creature did a few more loop-de-loops before jerking to a halt inches from Kristian's crossed eyes.

"Why are you pestering us? Leave us alone." Gracie rested her hands on his shoulders and peeked around his head. Her breath tickled his ear.

The creature's bright yellow wings were the size of a hummingbird's and purred like a kitten. Its striped, multicolored tights clung to its scrawny legs, which dangled beneath a pointy-hemmed purple dress. It moved its legs as if treading water. A long, red ponytail hung past its bare feet with bangs that swooped to one side, partially covering a sky blue eye. Kristian decided it was female.

Without warning, she thumped Kristian's forehead with her

tiny fist. He threw his head back and hit Gracie's forehead again.

"That's it." She barged around him, almost knocking him down, and shoved her long, slender finger at the tiny creature. "You listen here, whoever you are. Leave us alone before I—" She swatted at the creature buzzing around them. "Go on, get away—"

Before his sister finished her sentence, the creature thumped her forehead. Gracie jerked backward.

"Why you little nymph." She blew out her cheeks like a pufferfish.

Kristian knew she was about to lose it. He grabbed her arm. "Come on. Let's just go, and maybe she'll go away."

She batted at the tiny, buzzing creature as he tugged her arm. The creature followed along and halted in front of them. In a squeaky voice, the creature said, "HadToGetYourAttention. Come."

Gracie squinted and pursed her lips. "Why you little—I'll get your attention all right." She swatted at the creature, who zipped this way and that, shooting back and forth to escape the girl's wrath. "HurryCome."

"Who are you?" Kristian asked.

"Dixie.IMeanYouNoHarm.WantToSeeWhatHappened ToYourDad, yes? IShowYou. Come."

They froze. The creature zipped around them. "Come, IShowYou."

"Kristian, I don't have a good feeling about this little nymph." Gracie rubbed her forehead. "Let's just go back to the castle."

"Don't you want to know what happened to Dad?" His muscles

tightened. "I'm going to follow her. You can go back if you want."

His stomach curled into a knot as he hobbled cautiously after the little sprite, secretly hoping Gracie would follow. If she didn't, he might decide against it too.

"Wait." Gracie caught up. He sighed but grinned without Gracie seeing.

Kristian flicked thin, overgrown limbs out of their way as they traipsed along the worn path behind Dixie, who zipped behind a high waterfall. The cool mist swooped around them as they followed her into a chilly, damp cave.

"HurryCome." Dixie zipped farther into the cave.

Farther along, Kristian heard Elliott's hooves at the entrance. "Come back, Elliott called.

He hesitated and glanced back. But he reached for Gracie's hand and scooted farther into the cave behind Dixie. If it hadn't been for the creature's tiny, glowing light, it would have been pitch black.

Kristian glanced back again, but all he could see was a small, dim light waving around the entrance. He stopped and stared at it. It looked like the veiled light, blinking and dashing about, as if it were warning him of something.

"I have a bad feeling about this." Gracie's hand trembled against his arm.

"But if Dixie knows where Dad is, we need to follow her. If you want to go back, then go." He held his breath.

"Okay, I'll go. But we're making a big mistake."

He exhaled. The smell of wet rock and moss drifted through

the cave as Dixie twittered deeper down the narrow passageway. Now she looked like a tiny, green glow stick. Kristian groped along the damp wall, as they tottered across rocky ground and then a small bridge with trickling water. The air was still and chilly.

He walked into a spider web, which gave him the creeps, and then Gracie grabbed his shirt and crumpled it into a wad. He glanced back at the entrance. The veiled light was gone.

"Maybe we should—" He wiped his forehead.

"Kristian—" Elliott's voice echoed.

"Hurry. GrabMyPonyBraid. We must time travel."

Time travel? Kristian held his breath before they both screamed. They floundered downward. Cold air rushed past them as if falling into a bottomless pit. They landed and tumbled across the plump ground. Kristian rubbed his eyes and peeped through some flimsy, weeping willow limbs rustling in a small breeze. The sun's rays glimmered across a lake. He stood and rushed from under the tree but bounced backward.

Gracie reached down and helped him up. "It's some kind of barrier. We're stuck."

"Look—it's Dad." Kristian rammed the barrier, harder this time, but it sent him reeling backward.

Their dad clanked tackle boxes inside a small dented rowboat.

This time Gracie took aim and ran into the barrier. She bounced back and knocked Kristian down. He nudged her off and punched the barrier.

"Listen," Gracie said.

"Come on, kids, the fish won't wait forever," their dad called.

They stared as their dad clattered fishing poles and sang their favorite childhood song. "There's a hole in my bucket, Dear Liza, Dear Liza. There's a hole in my bucket, Dear Liza, a hole. Then mend it, Dear Henry, Dear Henry, Dear Henry. Then mend it, Dear Henry, Dear Henry, mend it."

"Dad," Kristian screamed.

"He can't hear us," Gracie said. "This is all your fault. I told you not to follow the little nymph."

"You came too." They clawed at the barrier until Kristian's fingertips burned. Finally, the barrier ripped. "Come on!"

They dashed around the lake toward their dad. Gracie grabbed Kristian's arm and jerked him to a stop. "Wait. Look." She flung her hand over her mouth and pointed with her other hand. "Beside that tree—it's me."

"Kristian," their dad called. Kristian gawked when he noticed himself hobble across the glen toward the lake. The veiled light swept around on the other side of the lake, as if trying to warn them.

Then a loud screeching sound ripped through the forest. The kids covered their ears.

"That's the sound I heard the day dad disappeared," Kristian said.

"I heard it, too." Gracie twisted the bottom of his shirt.

"Elliott tried to rescue you that day." Kristian pointed. "It's SanDorak. And someone's riding her, but I can't make out who it is." He cupped his hands around his mouth. "Dad, look out!"

As they raced around the lake, the veiled light drew closer.

"He can't hear us," Gracie shouted.

SanDorak dove toward their dad and plucked him off the ground. The tips of her black-ribbed wings whipped the pine branches and hurled limbs along her path.

"You said you didn't know what happened to Dad that day. How could you not have remembered this?" He glared at his sister. "You hate lies."

Gracie shook her head. "No, I promise I didn't lie. I must have blocked it from my mind. But now I remember. That beast chased dad, and they disappeared into the forest, headed toward that old tree."

Kristian noticed the veiled light darting all over. "Do you see that light?"

She shoved her hair out of her eyes. "Where?"

"Never mind, let's go." They rushed toward the forest's edge. A grisly sound ripped through the forest, and Kristian jerked to a halt.

"W-what was t-that?" Gracie's eyes bulged.

"I told you. I tried telling all of you about the creature that roamed the forest, but no one believed me."

"Okay, I believe you. What is it?"

The shadow growled louder as it slithered through the trees and swirled to a stop at the edge of the forest. Its lime green eye darted around as if looking for its prey.

Kristian grabbed his sister's arm and tugged her down into some weeds. "It never goes past the forest edge." He wheezed as icy fear gripped him like a python. "Come on."

He gripped Gracie's hand and ran parallel along the forest wall. The shadow growled as it followed along inside the forest. They slammed into another barrier and shot backward.

"We have to break through this barrier if we're going to reach dad," he shouted.

"Find dad?" Gracie yelled. "Are you crazy? We have to get out here."

"I'm not leaving until we get him."

"Then you'll get him by yourself because I'm not go—"

The sky opened and poured rain. The wind gusted. SanDorak emerged from the dark belly of the forest, rushing past the shadow until it disappeared in the distance.

"Why isn't the shadow chasing SanDorak?" she asked.

Kristian heard Mikal's voice shouting through the blowing, pouring rain. "There they are."

"It's Mikal and Elliott." Kristian's legs wobbled as he and Gracie ran in the opposite direction. "Come on, this way."

He tripped, and they rolled across the gushy ground. She grabbed his arm and flung it around her neck, helping him to his feet. Elliott swooped down, and Mikal yanked them both off the ground, one at a time. They sped off through the dense gray clouds.

"Elliott, Dad's down there. He needs our help." Kristian kicked Elliott's sides, trying to escape Mikal's clutches. "Get your hands off me."

The Friesian streaked over the mountains, back through the portal, and raced through the universe.

Gracie managed to free herself from Mikal's grasp. "Don't touch me."

"I warned you it wasn't safe on Earth," Elliott said. "If we hadn't rescued you, you would've been trapped between two worlds."

"But—our dad." Kristian heaved in and out, as he shoved his hair off his forehead. He glanced around for Dixie, but she had vanished.

"What even happened?" Gracie asked.

"Dixie brought you back in time," Elliott said, "but there's a barrier that separated you from the past. Even if you could have broken that barrier, your father wouldn't have been able to see or hear you. Penetrating the line between the past and present would've only imprisoned you. I'm not sure if Dixie took you back there to show you what happened that day or to cause trouble."

Kristian rubbed his eyes with the balls of his hands and hung his head. "How did you find us?"

"When I spotted you following Dixie into the cave, I figured what she was up to. You're not the only ones she's taken back to Earth. So, Mikal and I went through the portal in the great tree in the forest, hoping we could rescue you in time."

EIGHT

Elliott's hooves clicked on the courtyard of Mighty Loft, and Sabrina walked briskly toward them. "Where've you been? You're soaking wet."

Kristian and Gracie slid to the ground. Kristian squatted next to Elliott's front leg and leaned back, hugging his knees and squeezing his eyes shut. "Dixie said we'd find our dad." His heart felt heavy in his chest.

"That pesky little sprite." Sabrina shook her head. "She never gives up. I do wish she'd stop bothering innocent beings. You cannot trust her, not even for a micro second."

Half-dazed, Kristian rested his forehead on his knees. His head ached.

Gracie sighed.

Out of the corner of his eye, Kristian saw her shake her head. He could feel her stare, the same stare she always gave when she blamed him for something.

"Come on, sweetie." Sabrina nudged Gracie with her nose. They headed toward the stables. "Let's go for a stroll until we can all calm down."

Kristian felt a few warm drops of water on his head.

Thinking it was rain, he glanced up. To his surprise, he

discovered the drops were coming from Elliott.

"What's wrong?" He stroked the horse's wet nose.

"I almost didn't get to you in time." A thin string of snot dribbled from his nose and splattered on the ground. "You can't allow that little nymph to deceive you like that again. Our enemies deceive us when we want something so badly that we let our guard down. We must guard our hearts and our emotions."

Kristian nodded. "I don't see why anyone would want to go back in time to some event that they can't change and take a chance of getting stuck there." He rested his head on his knees. "Now I'll never know what happened to my dad."

Elliott slid his warm, smooth tongue across the side of Kristian's head. A mixture of light and dark clouds drifted across the sky. Darker clouds crept upward along the planet's perimeter. The planet looked strange: the rainbow was fading, the wormhole was shrinking, and the land was growing a darker gray, like a black and white TV program.

When he'd calmed down, Kristian followed Mikal into the castle's alcove in the foyer, staring at the white book as he slowly hobbled past. He figured that book held the answers to his questions.

"This way." Mikal led him down a curved hall. When they reached the Great Room, atop a dais was a high-backed throne with a bright red cushion. Behind the throne an enormous oval-shaped window with a large rectangular stained glass window on each side. A kaleidoscope of colors sprayed across the white ceramic floor, and a small fire crackled in the fieldstone fireplace displayed from floor to ceiling.

"Where is everyone?" he asked as he glanced around the room.

"Come on." The slender man darted up the grand staircase two steps at a time and waited at the top.

Kristian slid his hand across the dull rail and hobbled up the steps. Halfway up, he stopped and stared at the portrait on the floral-patterned wall—a king and queen. The king's amber eyes looked familiar. He looked like the same man sitting atop Elliott in the white book. Kristian held his breath for a second; below the king's left ear was a mole. He'd noticed the mole earlier but hadn't thought about how it was in the same place as his own.

"Weird." He ran his finger across his own mole beneath his left ear. "Who are they?"

"King Malakon and Lady Grace." Mikal trounced back down the stairs. "I was seven when my parents died. The king and his lady were kind enough to take me in and care for me."

He could relate, as far as knowing the devastation of losing a father, but a mother too… He shuddered just thinking of it.

Mikal dashed up the stairs and disappeared around the corner, opening and closing doors. He stormed out of the room and rushed back down the stairs, jumping three steps at a time until he reached the bottom. "He's gone—I knew it."

"Maybe he's in the gardens." Kristian followed Mikal down the stairs and back into the great room. He caught Gerwin peeking around the kitchen doorway.

"No. He hates the gardens. Elliott! Sabrina!"

Kristian stopped at the doorway to the courtyard. He flicked his eyes at the white book and took a deep breath. While Mikal rushed outside, he hobbled toward the book, opened it, and skimmed the pages.

"What do you two know of the king's disappearance?" he heard Mikal ask the Friesians through the doors.

He drew a breath. On one of the pages, he noticed a wooden desk and a diamond box on top with its lid askew. The desk stood behind four white-ribbed pillars that reached from floor to ceiling in a semicircular alcove with a dome ceiling. There was a mural of a forest, a stream, and some mountains on the wall behind the desk.

Leaning closer, he noticed a small, silver skeleton key nestled inside the diamond box. His heart fluttered. "A key?" Could that be *the* key? He flipped the page. It was blank.

Kristian rushed outside. Sabrina was in Mikal's face. "And furthermore, who appointed you overseer of us? We are Dia's guardians, not you."

"And besides, I wasn't here." Elliott glared at Sabrina. "Just where were you, anyway?"

"I don't believe that is any of your concern." She pushed her nose toward him. "I didn't see or hear anything unusual."

Elliott clopped toward Kristian and whispered in his ear. "She's steamed. I went too far."

Mikal paced, murmuring several times. "What have I done?" He clutched his head.

"Excuse me?" Sabrina stomped over to him, and he jerked to a halt. "Do tell us, what *have* you done?"

He rested his hands on his hips, turned his back to Sabrina, and glanced into space. His face turned a milky white. Kristian followed his gaze. There were three black spheres way out in the universe. Each sphere had a different colored circle around it. One circle was blue, one was red, and one green.

Sabrina sighed and turned to Elliott. "I think we need to check out Zorak and look for Ruben."

Sirus waddled up and stood beside Kristian. "All the spheres continue to change places with the others, so we don't really know which leads to Zorak."

"I think I'll stay here and watch over Dia." Elliott turned in a half circle and trotted off, but Sabrina stopped him by nipping his mane.

"No you don't. You'll go with us." She turned to Sirus. "I think we should go as soon as possible."

"Where's Zorak?" Kristian and Gracie asked in unison.

Sabrina explained that Malakon had exiled Ruben to Zorak to prevent him from taking their father's throne. "And he's had it in for him ever since."

Elliott shook his head and ruffled his mane.

"Ruben may have returned and kidnaped Malakon." Mikal wiped his nose.

Kristian wondered if the diamond box might be on Zorak. "I'm going with you guys."

"I think we should stay here," Gracie said firmly.

"You can stay, but I'm going." His heart fluttered, and he took a deep breath.

She shook her head. "You're impossible. Someone has to keep an eye on you; it might as well be me."

He exhaled but then responded, "I don't need a baby-sitter." Why had he said that?

"Oh, I think you do."

Kristian turned and saw other Dians standing across the courtyard, murmuring among themselves. It was the first large crowd of them he'd seen since he'd been here—children and adults—and they all had blond hair and blue eyes.

Mikal jumped on a rock and raised his hand. The murmurs stopped. He placed his hands on his hips and scanned the crowd. His hair was out of control as if a windstorm had hit. His face was pale.

"I'm sorry to say the king is missing." Loud murmurs arose, and he wiped his lips with a trembling hand. "If anyone knows his whereabouts, please, make haste, and come forward."

"What happened?" someone called out.

"I'm not sure. Ruben may have taken him." More gasps. He raised his hand. "He could be on Lia, our sister planet. We'll check there too."

The mumbling crowd dispersed. Sirus tugged on Kristian's pant leg with his teeth.

"What is it?" He leaned down to hear what the little donkey wanted to say.

"Ramón is Ruben's and Malakon's father and the king of Lia,

that shining planet out there." Sirus nodded. "He promised that his firstborn son, which is Ruben, would be heir to his kingdom. Malakon didn't want that. He felt like he was better equipped for such an honor—"

Mikal interjected. "Malakon claims he's the firstborn and that the kingdom belongs to him."

"Malakon's jealousy has grown into rage," said Sirus.

"And for good reason," the man snapped. "He *is* the firstborn. Plus, Ramón gave Ruben a golden heart that supposedly holds a power so strong it can save Dia from the darkness that's falling over the planet, but Ruben claimed he had no such heart."

Kristian tried to swallow the golf ball-sized lump in his throat. He slid his hand into his pocket and clutched the golden heart. What were the chances of two identical golden hearts in the universe? He glanced at Gracie. She stared at him as if she knew he was up to something. He was dying to tell her, but he couldn't.

"Dia is growing darker by the hour." Elliott clopped up. "And we are growing weaker."

Mikal eyed Kristian. "Do you know anything about a golden heart?"

Kristian flicked his eyes at Elliott and cringed. "I...I'm not into jewelry."

Gracie's breath tickled the back of his neck as she whispered, "You know something, don't you?"

He tugged on Elliott's mane and pulled him aside, but she followed. Kristian glanced at her. "Do you mind?"

She shrugged. "No, I don't. What do you know?"

He leaned close to Elliott's ear. "Does Zorak have a castle?"

"Yes, why?"

Sabrina clopped toward them, so Kristian remained silent.

But he'd search for the diamond box and key when they arrived.

NINE

Elliott tossed two slobbery apples at the twins. They wiped them off and bit into the sweet, meaty, red balls. Kristian chomped and slurped while Gracie savored each bite.

The stallion moved his head toward Sirus. "I do hope you're staying here while we go to Zorak. You'll only be in the way."

"Sorry, but I go where Kristian goes."

"If we run into SanDorak, she'll squish you like a bug." Elliott snarled his top lip and then winked at Kristian. "Sure, do come along."

Sirus glared at him. "You're afraid of her."

"Utter nonsense." The Friesian snorted and walked off. But his legs quivered.

Kristian glanced at the group that would accompany him to Zorak. Sabrina was charming and protective; Elliott, clumsy, yet willing to risk his life if need be; Sirus, mysterious, wise, but somewhat of a scaredy-cat; and then there was Mikal, secretive, assertive, and conceded. They knew the universe better than he did and were his best hope of getting to Zorak and finding the key.

The breeze whipped Linnea's long curls around her shoulders as she stood poised near the fountain in the courtyard with her hands clasped behind her back. Her rose scent drifted in the wind, causing Kristian's skin to tingle.

"Is she coming along?" he asked Mikal as he nodded toward Linnea.

Mikal shook his head. "No."

It felt like someone deflated Kristian's lungs.

***

Elliott and Sabrina glided under Dia's Grand Arch with Kristian and the others. It glistened like stone coated with sugar and divided Dia's inner and outer limits. Elliott passed through the arch and low hanging clouds.

Kristian's eyes widened when he noticed a seventeenth-century ship docked alongside a giant pier at the edge of Dia. The Dians had already begun filling the ship with supplies. The smell of timber wafted past them. Their mumbles swept through the fog. He wasn't good at guessing measurements, but he figured the vessel had to be at least the length of four football fields and at least two football fields wide. The bow was copper, and the bowsprit had been delicately carved into the image of a dove. Burned into the hull was the name *Cosmic Star*.

The Friesian's hooves thumped onto the deck. Sabrina stretched her wing and kept Elliott from falling when he stumbled on a coiled rope. Kristian tasted sea salt on his lips. When he glanced beneath the vessel, he noticed that it was floating…in space.

He gazed at the striped tan and alabaster sails as he slid off Elliott, rushed to stern, and studied the navigational instrument panel that he had learned was an astrolabe. He took a deep breath as his mind wandered back to the time he and his family visited his cousins on the North Sea near the River Spey. Those times were some of his favorite.

"Look." Gracie pointed to a flock of miniature, jade-colored birds flitting around the sails.

Sabrina sighed. "Oh, our dear little Pippins. They'll be moving this great vessel, you know."

"Them?" Kristian scrunched his nose as they swooped up and down around the sails. "Aren't they a bit small for that?"

"Nonsense. You shall be surprised when you see how small creatures can do some pretty amazing things up here." She whistled, and five Pippins flitted down and landed on his shoulder. He glared at them out of the corner of his eye.

Gracie bounced on her tiptoes, like a child peeking over a fence to glimpse at the circus elephants. Her eyes lit up. "They're awesome."

He shook his head. She always brought strays home that their parents would later have to release into the wild. She thought they had always escaped.

"Strange." Mikal furrowed his brows. "They've never gotten this close to a stranger." A muscle twitched in Kristian's face as the man narrowed his gaze.

Sabrina smiled. "I'd say that makes him unique."

"Yeah, as unique as a skunk," Gracie muttered, spouting a tiny giggle.

Kristian smirked. The tiny creatures marched sideways down his arm, pricking him with their micro-sized claws. "Ouch."

They stopped in a line on his arm, and he studied them out of the corner of his eye. They had a red dot above each of their bright blue eyes. Their pale yellow beaks curved slightly, and their wings looked like weeping willow leaves. He reached out and barely touched one of the creature's white, fan-like tail before the rest fluttered back to the sails.

Elliott tromped across the deck.

"How'd this ship get here?" Kristian asked.

"It's just always been here," Elliott said.

Dark clouds inched up around Dia's perimeter. Kristian shivered as he stood next to Gracie on the starboard side, observing the stars that glistened even more than on Earth. For the first time since he'd been here, he wasn't feeling homesick.

"I hope we don't run into any—" Mikal lumbered toward them.

"Mikal," Sabrina snapped.

He turned and stomped off.

"Run into what?" Kristian glanced at Sabrina, who eyed the man as he disappeared below deck. He glanced over the hull. "How does this ship sail when there's no water?"

"The Cosmic River," Elliott said.

Gracie stared at a towering nebula filled with every color one could imagine. "I don't see any river."

"Come, Elliott." Sabrina trotted down the deck and jumped into the air, and he followed. They circled the Grand Arch, soared through a nebula, and into the universe out of sight. Moments later, they returned carrying between their teeth a huge multicolored swath like a glittery ribbon. It waved like a silk scarf and was as wide as the ship. They each slipped their end beneath the ship—Elliott at the stern, Sabrina at the bow. The ship lurched, bobbed, and squeaked against the pier.

Gracie grabbed Kristian's shirt and jerked him from his grip on the hull. They floundered across the deck and became tangled in a net. Sirus slid past them. Kristian gripped his tail on the way by, but Sirus still slid into a capstan and released a grunt. The vessel tottered.

A cowbell clanked. Then it clanked again only louder.

"Uh, oh." Elliott flicked his wings.

"What's that noise?" Sabrina asked.

"Uh...no need for alarm. Everything's...under control." He bumbled and swayed, and the whites of his eyes widened as he turned his head every-which-way.

"Under control, huh?" Kristian blurted. "Looks like you're the only one who's alarmed.

"Uh..." Elliott gulped. He finally found his footing. "Whew. I'm okay." The sound didn't return.

The Cosmic River sparkled in a colorful array like the noonday sun on Lake Superior. The river was as wide as the Grand Canyon and flowed upward at a forty-five degree incline toward the three distant color rings lined in a row.

"This river is really weird." By now, Gracie had gotten to her feet and clung to the hull. "Seems like a gazillion, micro-sized, cosmic particles are holding this ship up. How can a river flow upstream, anyway?"

"Even weirder," Kristian wondered aloud, "how can anything float on this stuff?"

The river disappeared into the darkness. There was a chill in the air. Elliott and Sabrina tossed the mooring ropes onto the pier and set sail.

Kristian got goosebumps when he noticed Linnea standing beneath the grand arch watching as they sailed away. Those goosebumps also quivered across his heart.

In the distance, above Dia, he noticed the veiled light's faint glow floating near the wormhole. It disappeared and reappeared in and out of the wormhole several times; again, it was as if it were trying to tell him something. But what?

TEN

A fairy-type creature whizzed past Kristian's head. He ducked. "Whoa, not another pixie."

Sabrina smiled. "Not to worry, it's only Meme."

Meme jerked to a halt. She stood stiff at attention in front of Mikal's face. She saluted. "Ready and waiting, sir."

Her squeaky voice sounded military-like. Several bright, red braids stuck out from the top of her floppy, dark teal hat, making them look like a rooster's tail. Fixed to the front of the hat was a tiny, yellow daisy. Her blue-and-purple striped dress ruffled in the breeze over the white and dark green, striped tights that covered her sprout legs.

She zipped back to the others, leaving a fresh, starchy scent in the air.

"What was that?" Kristian and Gracie said in unison.

"She's in charge of the Pippins." Sabrina smiled.

"You'll do well staying out of her way," Mikal warned. "She's a pest, that one."

"She just likes to run a tight ship." Sabrina peered at him. "Nothing wrong with that. She has little patience for mischief. And she doesn't take kindly to anyone who tries to harm her Pippins."

Meme cleared her throat. "Okay, Pippins, heads up. Fall in line. Ta-ta!"

She raised her small, slender arms as her tiny wings hummed. The Pippins' wings sounded like soft, buzzing flies as they weaved around the sails.

After finding their spots, Meme zipped back to Mikal, stopping inches from his nose. With a salute, she said, "Ready and waiting, sir."

He swatted at her. "Must you always salute me and talk to me like that? Just get us going, will you?" He sauntered to the helm.

Her little head drooped, and her shoulders slumped as she floated in the air, staring at the deck in a bit of a daze before meandering back toward the Pippins.

"That Mikal, he doesn't care what he says or who he hurts sometimes." Sabrina sighed. "Meme is so eager to help."

Kristian whistled, and Meme stopped. When she turned, he motioned for her. She fluttered back to him like a drifting feather, head still drooping, shoulders still slumping, and stopped in front of him. He lifted her tiny chin with the tip of his pinky finger and stared into her miniature, turquoise eyes.

"Pay no attention to him," he whispered. "You're a brave little pixie. And he's a bully. Just keep doing what you do best."

She fluttered her dark lashes as if sprouting back to life. The corner of her mouth lifted, and she smiled from one tiny ear to the other, as her eyes grew bright. She took a deep breath, straightened her posture, and saluted. Kristian saluted her back and winked.

As she zipped back to the Pippins, her dress ruffled in the breeze. "Ta, ta, ladies. Steady as we go. Zing-zing. Zing-zang-zing. Zang-zing-zang. Onward!"

The Pippins joined the glee and twirled, swirled, and whirled around the sails. He grinned and winked at Meme, who winked back. The vessel dipped, bobbed, and creaked up the Cosmic River toward the unknown reaches of an unknown galaxy.

Kristian chewed his fingernail. He didn't know how anyone could be excited and woozy at the same time, but he sure was. Sailing was not his best friend, but he enjoyed it.

Elliott stood at the bow while Sabrina stood astern. When they laid their wings to their sides, it was almost an illusion because their wings blended in until they almost disappeared.

Gracie twisted a strand of loose hair around her finger as she gazed into the heavens. "Look."

Hazy colors of orange, lavender, blue, yellow, and pink spheres hung scattered in an array of majestic splendor, planets that no one had known existed far from a telescope's prying eyes. Farther ahead, more nebulae sprouted into view like giant, vibrant pillars of purples, reds, and pastels. Kristian's stomach twittered.

Sirus waddled up. "Makes you want to believe that someone created all of this, doesn't it?"

"So you think someone did create all of this?"

"What do you think?"

Kristian really wasn't sure, although he wanted to believe it.

"Take the wheel and keep it steady," Mikal told Kristian. "I'll be back."

"But I don't know how to sail—"

"Just keep a tight grip." Sirus smiled. "It nearly sails itself."

As he gripped the moist, gritty wheel, the beastly vessel sailed smoothly up the river. His mind drifted to another time when his family visited his cousins in Scotland and their boat veered off course in the fog. Luckily, they weren't far from shore, but the fog had crept in so rapidly that they couldn't see a quarter of a mile ahead of them. It petrified him, but luckily, their parents found them.

A faint light in the distance caught his attention before it wavered and disappeared. "Did you see that?"

Elliott swerved his head in one direction and then the other. "See what?"

"You saw it, right?" Kristian glanced at Sirus, who nodded. "Why's it following us? I thought we left it back on Dia."

"It goes where it wants for reasons only it knows. It seems it was trying to tell you something, but you weren't listening."

"What do you mean?"

Just then, Mikal returned and grabbed the wheel. Sirus waddled off, and Kristian climbed down from the helm. For some reason, his foot wasn't aching. He spent a few minutes talking to Gracie and then slid his fingers across the hull's grainy surface and hobbled down a narrow hallway that led below deck.

He found a rusty door handle. He turned the squeaky knob and peered inside a dim room. Soft light filtered through rectangular windows, spraying its light across the dusty floor. It looked like the captain's cabin. The air was chilly, but sweat beaded across his forehead. He was trespassing into somebody's space.

A small, four-posted bed covered with a patchwork quilt of

reds, browns, and yellows, and a faded, flat, white pillow occupied the left side of the room. An antique wooden desk stood in the middle of the room. On top, a weathered ship's log, an empty oil lamp, and a map spread across the desk. The ship lurched, causing him to stumble and fall into a tattered brown leather chair. The chair's wheels squeaked as it rolled and bumped into an oak cabinet.

Kristian heard thumping sounds. He got up, tiptoed down a dark hallway where the noise came from, and pressed his ear against the cool, rough door. Several loud thumps hit the floor. His heart pounded as he gripped the doorknob and held his breath.

"Help!"

He flung open the door. "Sirus?"

"Hurry, my back." He was on the floor squirming.

"What are you doing in here?"

"No time—just scratch."

"You were into my blueberries," he said as he scratched his little friend fast and hard. His backpack was feet from them and half-hidden under a small bed. Blueberries were strewn.

A flash of light blitzed the room. The ship tilted, and Sirus bumbled as he tried to scramble to his hooves. "What was that?"

Kristian rushed out the door and slid across some slimy substance. A giant, cosmic wave had crashed over the hull and deposited a fluorescent green mixture. The vessel tilted and drenched them.

Mikal jerked his arms as he struggled with the wheel.

The ship vibrated. Kristian thought it would bust the bulkheads.

Another wave crashed over the side.

"My skin is stinging." Kristian tried wiping it off, but it was like thick goo.

The ship tilted the other way. The wheel spun and knocked Mikal's feet out from under him, throwing him off the helm.

"Kristian!" Gracie spun around one of the pole masts as she gripped the pole. Cosmic fireballs the size of softballs rained down onto the deck like hail splattering, hissing, and sizzling. "Someone make it stop."

"We're the only someones up here." Kristian reached into his pocket and squeezed the golden heart. He gulped and took a deep breath. "Meme—"

"Pippins," Meme shouted. "Ta, ta!"

The little birds twirled and swirled until they formed a giant, green blur around the entire vessel like a spider web. The cosmic fireballs bounced off.

Sirus's tail got caught around Kristian's foot, jerking him off his feet. They both slid across the deck and tumbled over the side of the hull just as the ship tipped.

"Elliott! Save them!" Kristian heard Gracie's garbled pleas and saw a bulging vein on Mikal's forehead, shaped like a V just before he slipped beneath the glimmering river.

Bubbles gurgled from Sirus's mouth as Kristian wiped his burning eyes. He watched Elliott's and Sabrina's blurry images with their necks stretched over the side of the ship as he sank deeper. Why weren't they jumping in to save them?

When he turned his head, he spotted the golden heart floating through the colored particles. He flicked and flailed to reach it, but back-waved his hands when he spotted two milky-white eyes trimmed in scarlet staring at him and slithering toward him.

It was a giant, mother-of-all electrical eels. Its beady eyes glared at him with cold contempt, and its body sparked as it slithered in for the kill.

Kristian flailed his arms and legs. The creature squirmed this way and that. It whipped its tail through the river particles. Every nerve in his body burned as the creature's eyes ignited in flames. Razor-sharp teeth protruded from its large, fat-lipped mouth. It darted toward him as he tried in a desperate attempt to escape, kicking his legs until he lost feeling in them.

The creature clamped its teeth on his pant leg, ripping the material, just grazing his calf. His leg stung like fire as it dragged him through the river.

Just as he was about to black out, he felt an arm clutch his chest and jerk him. He saw the blurry image of the headless body of the creature float past them. However, something heavy still clung to his leg. When he glanced down, he saw the creature's head with its razor-sharp teeth still attached to his pant leg.

He jerked his leg to release the creature's head as his sister tugged him toward the vessel where a rope was waiting. Gracie tied the rope around both of them while Mikal hauled them up the side. At the top of the hull, Mikal pried the creature's mouth from Kristian's pants.

Then everything went black.

Kristian woke to Sabrina's hooves pumping his chest. He choked and heaved as the stinging particles rushed up his throat and through his nose, spraying Gracie's face.

"Yuck." She threw a bucket of water on him and Sirus.

Kristian sat up and coughed the bitter substance until he gagged. He glared at the Friesians. "Why didn't you guys save us? We could've died."

"Whoa," Elliott said. "Calm down."

"Calm down?" Kristian flung his arms in the air. "We could've died."

"I'm afraid we can't swim in that stuff." Sabrina hung her head. "It's too heavy for our wings."

He ran his hand through his sticky hair. He felt awful for getting mad. "I'm sorry. I didn't know."

Mikal spread a yellow salve over Kristian's leg, wrapped it in a white cloth, and strode off.

"Oh, no." Kristian patted his pant pocket. He grasped Sirus's ear and limped away from the others. "I never got the heart back."

Sirus's shoulders moved slightly.

"It's not funny."

He spread his lips. Nestled between his teeth was the heart. Irritated, Kristian pinched the heart between his fingers and yanked, stretching Sirus's lip.

"Ouch! Why'd you do that?"

Kristian hung his head and shoved the heart in his pocket. "I'm sorry. I should be thankful to you for saving me." His heartbeat went back to normal as he traipsed down the deck to the captain's cabin and dropped on the lumpy mattress. The stinging in his leg had subsided.

He slipped the torn piece of paper from his pocket that he had picked up in the forest back on Earth. The words read, "Guard the heart." What could it mean?

Next, he pulled out the family photo and ran his thumb across his dad's face. He remembered the nights they camped beneath the stars. He could almost smell the pan-fried fish and hear the gentle water lap against the shore.

He closed his eyes and drifted off to sleep.

ELEVEN

The next morning, Kristian stood at the bow with Gracie while Mikal maneuvered the speeding vessel farther upriver. A coral planet glowed with a hint of speckles, casting a faint bronze off the twinkling stars.

Gracie slapped the hull. "Look."

Three immense, galactic wormholes revolved like cylinder tubes ahead. Kristian absentmindedly squeezed her shirt. Mikal stared at the wormholes as if he had seen three sea monsters. Sirus shivered against Kristian's leg. They looked threatening.

He glanced down and caught Sirus staring at him. "What are you looking at?"

"Your journey is about to get complicated."

"What do you mean?"

"Do you remember seeing a clue in the white book that might help us know which sphere to take? None of us knows which sphere is the correct one because they keep changing positions."

"How am I supposed to know which one it is?" His heartbeat managed to make its way into his throat. Sirus trembled. "What's wrong?"

"Choose incorrectly, and another dimension could gobble us up, and we may never see the light of day again."

Gracie stomped her foot. "Since this is your so-called journey, I suggest you figure something out."

"Pipe down. Let me think." He bit a fingernail and paced along the side of the hull, staring at the wormholes. He stretched his collar away from his neck, and tried to remember what he'd seen in the book that could give him a clue. "I don't know which one it is."

"Well, I can't help you." She glared at him. "You and Sirus were the only one who could see what was on the pages."

Sirus scuffed his hoof on the deck. "Listen to your heart."

"I doubt my heart's going to save us. We don't have time for nonsense like that. If we go through the wrong sphere—" He hobbled down the deck and darted into the captain's cabin. He dropped down on the bed, closed his eyes, and took deep breaths. "Think, think, think."

When he opened his eyes, he spotted the veiled light floating over the map on the desk. "Glad to see you could show up. Help me, won't you?"

It swooshed out of his way, flinging dust in the air. He coughed and brushed his hand across the map.

"Hurry up." Gracie barged into the room. The door clapped against the wall as the ship began to vibrate.

"Leave me alone for a minute." He scooted her out the door and slammed it shut. Fear gripped him as his eyes glossed over the map. He wiped the dust from his eyes and tried to remember some clue in the white book.

"You must hurry." Elliott shouted on the other side of the door. He kicked the door open and pushed his head through the opening.

"Would you guys leave me alone?"

"We're getting way too close," Elliott said.

Gracie and Sirus squirmed and squeezed through Elliott's legs. "What are you going to do?"

"Let me concentrate."

Everyone muttered and hustled back out the door. Gracie grunted and stomped out.

The timbers of the ship creaked.

Kristian glared at the crinkled map, paced, and tapped his head. "Think."

He swiped another swath of dust. This time he saw a white book in the upper right corner. There was a small image of a man sitting on a white horse, the same man he'd seen in the white book back on Mighty Loft. He swiped the remaining dust from the map.

There—three wormholes, each one with a different color circle: bright white, bright blue, and bright red.

Elliott, Gracie, and Sirus pushed their heads through the doorway again. "We're getting dangerously closer."

Kristian's surroundings faded, and his eyeballs ached. He bit his bottom lip and tasted a small tang of blood as he tapped his finger on the map. The red-ringed wormhole was bolder and thicker than the others. "This has to be the one."

The veiled light zipped around in the room as if panic-stricken, but he had no time to be pestered with it. He ignored it and ran out of the room.

"We're coming to the forks in the river," Mikal shouted from the helm. "We're heading right toward the white-ringed wormhole."

"No." Kristian pushed past the others and raced to the helm. "The red one. Go to the red one."

The three wormholes swirled and loomed ahead of them.

"Meme, stop the ship. Back us up."

"It's too late," Mikal shouted.

The veiled light swooshed across the bow toward the white wormhole. It wavered near the entrance.

Meme and the Pippins swooshed around the sails to try stopping the vessel, but their best efforts failed. "This has never happened before. The vacuum from the wormhole is too great. It's sucking us in."

Kristian shook as icy gusts of wind slapped against his face. He bumped Mikal out of the way and seized the wheel.

"It has to be the red-ringed sphere," he shouted at the veiled light.

"Who are you hollering at?" Sabrina and Elliott asked.

"Oh, no." Sirus widened his eyes.

The wheel vibrated, and Kristian's fingers cramped. As the vessel drew closer, Gracie grabbed the wheel and grunted, but it wouldn't budge. The vessel tilted and creaked until the wormhole swallowed them in its white and black mouth.

The horses' hooves clapped on deck as they paced from one end of the vessel to the other.

Mikal rushed astern. "We're going to die. I knew it."

"What do we do? We're doomed." Kristian's voice was stoical

with his last remark. He had failed—just like all the other times in his life.

Sabrina and Elliott nuzzled each other's neck. It became gravely quiet. Pitch-blackness buried the vessel. Kristian knew that everyone had succumbed to fear because of their silence. His temples throbbed. Gracie dug her fingernails into his arm, but he barely felt it.

TWELVE

The vessel lurched, swooshed, and plunged from the other side of the wormhole as if it had left the tracks of a roller coaster and dropped several feet. Darkness loomed. When the *Cosmic Star* found its sea legs once again, it drifted steadily toward a sound of swirling, thunderous water.

Elliott handed the children black capes, which they wrapped around them. A pain shot through Kristian's chest with each breath, and icy chips pricked his face. "Mikal, is this Zorak?"

"No."

The *Cosmic Star* creaked to halt. He slipped his hand into his pocket, gripped the golden heart, and took a deep breath. Gracie clung to his arm.

As if an atom exploded, trillions of lights shot through space like the Fourth of July and came to a sudden, glowing stop.

"Look, stars." His sister swiveled around and looked up. "It looks like an artist swung his paintbrush and spattered fluorescent white paint across a black canvas." Specks of light shone in her eyes. A huge smile graced Sirus's face.

The ship lurched and sailed toward the roaring water. The ride was as smooth as if it sailed on glass. A great, watery orb came into view. As the ship crept around the orb, three images appeared inside the orb: a mustard tree, a shield, and a bright light.

"What is that?" Kristian asked. Everyone stared as the vessel circled the orb. A warm rush spread through his body as he tried to figure out what the objects meant.

"The light shines on the darkness, and the darkness cannot overpower it," Sirus said. "But Dia's dying; time is short. I suppose that your journey had to be rushed. You must discover the mystery of these clues if you are to save Dia."

"I hate to interrupt your little dysfunctional gala here," Mikal spouted, "but I've had enough of this nonsense. Let's get out of here."

A boom shook the universe.

"It's easy to believe in things you can see." Sirus blinked. Kristian stared at the three objects as Mikal maneuvered the vessel back through the wormhole. "Many have not seen and still believe. It is this belief that grounds them and gives them hope and a persistence never to give up believing. Faith is what keeps people determined to keep going. More rewarded are those who believe and have not seen, than those who have seen and believe. Sadly, some never believe."

Kristian gazed at Sirus's peaceful face. It calmed him. He didn't know what he was supposed to believe, but he had a strong feeling that he was going to find out. Meme and the Pippins perched quietly on the masts as the vessel passed back through the wormhole's entrance. Kristian thought about the three objects and the mystery that surrounded them.

"There are two wormholes left, and one of them may be our end if you choose wrongly." Mikal tapped his finger on Kristian's chest. "Choose wisely."

"Alas, I believe a seed has sprouted in your heart," Sirus whispered as he waddled down the deck. "Now the final process can begin."

That little donkey knew something that he didn't. There were always hidden meanings to decipher up here.

The *Cosmic Star* sailed back down the river. Everyone acted as if they were in a daze after their little side trip. Kristian grew worried as the vessel picked up speed.

A giant cosmic wave broke the silence and crashed into the bow of the vessel, shooting it upward before slamming down on top of the waves.

"Slow us down," Gracie shouted and stomped her foot. "We're not going to make the turn." The vessel swiveled and tottered. She rushed in and tried wrestling Mikal's arm away from the wheel, but that only sent the wheel into a free spin.

Kristian lurched and grabbed the wheel. "Meme, we're heading for the edge."

"Ta-Ta, ladies. Quickly, find your sea-wings." Meme buzzed like an out-of-control fly. The Pippins became a green force as they swarmed the sails. The ship barely clung to the edge as the little birds swirled.

Kristian tried bumping Mikal out of the way as he tightened his grip on the wheel. "Move."

"Enough," Sabrina ordered. "Get this vessel under control."

Mikal jumped down and rushed off. The veiled light waved

near the red-ringed wormhole. Kristian squeezed the wheel until his knuckles ached. The ship's keel was the only thing preventing them from dropping off the river's edge. The bowsprit barely clung to the one o'clock position. Just as the ship tipped back the other way, Kristian snatched Sirus's tail before the donkey slid overboard, but Gracie's shirt twisted inside the wheel's casing.

"Get away."

"I can't. My shirt's stuck." She thrashed around while Kristian grunted and fought to release her shirt from the wheel. But the more the wheel spun, the tighter her top twisted into a wad. "Ouch! It's squeezing my belly."

If he spun the wheel in the opposite direction to untwist her shirt, the vessel would career off the edge of the river. He held his grip with one hand as he tried to rip her shirt from the casing with the other hand.

Elliott stepped in and gripped the wheel with his teeth. "Hurry!"

Her shirt tore, and she tumbled across the upper deck until she hit the hull. The wheel spun freely as if something snapped. Kristian tried to get control of it. Gracie raced over and grabbed the wheel, and they steadied the vessel with the help of the Pippins.

"Some navigator you are." She wheezed, trying to catch her breath. Her raggedy shirt rested just above her waist.

He glanced up at the veiled light as he gathered his wits. "I think we need to go that way. Can you handle the vessel for a minute?"

Gracie nodded. As the vessel sailed calmly down the river, he rushed past Elliott, Sabrina, and Sirus, feeling their eyes on him as he passed. He shut the door to the captain's cabin and dropped on the bed. He needed a few minutes to catch his breath.

He wished Nick and his dad were here. He couldn't understand why Dia was growing dark. Could the golden heart really save Dia? And what about the kings? Did they die? Get kidnapped?

He took a deep breath. Faith. What was faith, anyway? Sirus had explained it, but was it a feeling or something that comes over you? He didn't know, not yet.

Just as he was about to doze, he heard loud clanking.

"Oh, no. Not again." He shot off the bed and rushed out to the deck. He pounded his fist in the air. "Leave us alone."

SanDorak's black hide shone beneath the moon's pale glow as she soared over the vessel like a slow-moving airplane. She flicked the mizzenmast with the tip of her tail, scattering the Pippins in different directions. Gracie and Kristian stood at the helm, everyone frozen as they watched her circle the vessel. The monster disappeared into the red-ringed wormhole.

"This has to be the way, or she wouldn't have gone in there. Follow her," Kristian shouted.

The vessel entered the dark sphere. He could see the vague, dark image of SanDorak ahead of them like a stealth bomber. Her vast wings *whoomphed* through the tunnel and stirred the cold air that slapped his face with icy specks. She left a pungent odor in her wake, stinging his nostrils. He gripped his sword and shivered.

It was deathly quiet. No one talked. Even the Pippins remained silent.

He couldn't imagine what his mother's destiny was or what it had to do with Dia. Why did he have to fulfill her destiny? And the heart—how could such a tiny object have any power? What did it have to do with faith? He knew he couldn't ignore it. The thought wouldn't let go of him. He wiped his face, as he tried to stay focused on SanDorak.

But what about the kings? Was Mikal, Ruben, or Malakon involved in whatever happened to Aaron or Ramón? There was something Kristian knew for sure: he couldn't trust anyone, except maybe Linnea. She was friendly. He liked her. And deep down, he knew he could trust Gracie.

"Look." His sister jarred him back to his senses.

A small light near the end of the wormhole grew, as they got closer. They shot out the other side behind SanDorak and into a blinding blizzard. Kristian shivered as icy flakes clung to his eyelashes. He pulled his cape tighter. The *Cosmic Star* slammed into a giant snowdrift with a loud thud.

He wiped his eyes and tried to focus through the whiteout. He had a bad feeling about this place and wanted to leave. But if this was Zorak, he had to at least look for the key.

Mikal slung a net over his shoulders. "We'll need to get over that mountain range. The Friesians will have to walk us there."

Elliott led the way, trudging through the towering drifts, some as high as just beneath his chest. The wind howled and gusted. The planet shifted, and evergreen branches drooped.

Oddly enough, Kristian wasn't as cold as he had been. "How come I'm not cold?"

"Yeah, me either," Gracie added.

"That's impossible." Mikal peered at them. "It's at least ten below zero. Earthlings can't endure such temperatures without protection."

But Kristian barely heard him. He was busy staring at the icy daggers hanging from the cliffs.

Gracie buried her face into Sabrina's mane. "Why's the ground shaking?"

"Elliott." Sabrina pranced up beside him. They halted. "Did you feel that?"

"Yes." They pricked their ears forward.

"Is the planet going to explode?" Gracie asked.

"It's the rockmites." Sabrina and Elliott bolted through the drifts.

Kristian couldn't see anything. "What're rockmites?"

"Spiky creatures. They change color like chameleons and live underground. If they poke us, we'll turn to stone."

"That's just great," Kristian muttered.

The horses bounded up the mountain range, and the landscape shifted as if it melded into the planet's surface.

Kristian squinted through the wintry mix. "Is that the veiled light over there?" he asked Sirus.

"Seems a bit bright for the veil." Sirus peered through the white swirls.

"What are you two talking about?" Gracie stared in the same direction. "What are you looking at?"

"Let's go that way." The crisp air filled Kristin's lungs. "Stop."

He slid off Elliott and pulled Sirus with him. Sirus fell on top of him and smashed him into the snow. "Get off," Kristian mumbled. He shoved Sirus off, and all he could see were his long ears laying on top of the snow.

Elliott plucked the donkey up, shook him off along with Kristian, and set them back on his back. "I knew you'd be a nuisance." He eyed Sirus.

"Look. There's a light up ahead." Sabrina traipsed through the snow, and Elliott followed.

"I don't think that's the veiled light," he told Sirus. Kristian peered through the blizzard. "We're going the wrong way."

The planet shifted again.

"Listen." Elliott stopped. Mikal slid off Sabrina's back, yanked Kristian down off Elliott, and handed him one end of the net. "Take your end and secure it to one of those boulders over there. Hurry."

Kristian lumbered through the knee-deep snow, his clubfoot throbbing. The howling wind spit icy specks against his face. He stubbed his toe on a hidden boulder but ignored the pain. He hurled the net over the boulder but missed.

"Hurry," Mikal shouted.

"I'm trying." He turned. Black spikes poked through the snow and rolled toward them. Gracie screamed.

He hurled the net again, and this time snagged it on a pointy rock. The rockmites slammed into it, stretching the net several yards before they shot backward and bounded down the mountainside. The net snagged Kristian's foot and yanked him off his feet. Sleet pelted his face, stinging like bees, as he slid across the snow screaming.

SanDorak dove down from the gray sky to snatch him, but her talons became tangled in the net. She squawked as she flailed, trying to escape. Her wings swooshed as she bumbled down the mountainside, dragging him with her, and her tail whipped like an octopus's tentacles, lopping off masses of stiff, pine branches.

As she reached the bottom, she slid out of sight, and his foot released from the net. The impact forced him to slide several hundred yards in the opposite direction of SanDorak. He stopped when he rammed into something soft, yet firm.

"Not again," he groaned and lifted his head to try to focus past his frozen eyelashes. When his vision cleared, he followed the curvature of the creature's neck that towered above him, and into the most remarkable turquoise eyes he'd ever seen. The creature's coat was wispy bronze, and it had three melon-colored horns sticking from its forehead.

"Oh, gracious, are you okay?" said a gentle voice. "Please, you must free me before she gets up."

"You mean you know SanDorak?"

"Yes, and I'd say she's not really keen on me. Please, do hurry."

He stared at the real-life tri-corn. The creature shook her head, and a pile of snow dropped on the top his head.

"Please, do get me out of here before she wakes."

SanDorak lay moaning, tail sticking from a giant snow bank. Kristian plucked his sword from its sheath and with two hands began chipping the ice away from tri-corn's neck.

"I'm Aribella." She grunted. "I tumbled into this pond and couldn't free myself before the temperature dropped. It can happen suddenly here." She jerked her head back. "Careful with that."

"Sorry." Kristian heaved and grunted as he stabbed the ice. "I'm not...very good...with this yet."

The wet wind carried SanDorak's groans across the pond.

"Hurry. She'll be coming." Aribella's voice trembled.

SanDorak's thumps pounded the ice, and it quaked.

A jagged crack streaked between his feet. His legs stretched as the ice broke apart.

"Oh, dear. Grab one of my horns."

He grasped a horn just as one foot slid into the water. The tri-corn swung him and set him on the ice. Snow scrunched. SanDorak shot a stream of fire that just missed his head. She shot another. Kristian and Aribella ducked, but the stream of fire hit the ice and turned it into orange ice pellets, which rolled across the pond like marbles.

Another fiery streak bore into the ice around Aribella's neck, this time turning the ice into slush. She squirmed until she shot from her icy prison. She turned toward SanDorak and pointed her illuminated horns just as she approached.

The creature drew her legs to her chest and screeched. She

flicked her wings in a backward motion, but she still managed to puncture her thigh on Aribella's horn. Blood spurted onto the ice. The bloody pellets rolled like scattered pinballs. SanDorak slammed into the snowbank, but still managed to jump in the air and disappear into the pasty sky.

Gracie and the others bounded down the mountain and rushed up to Kristian. With a shaky voice, his sister held nothing back. "Just once in your life I wish you'd listen—just once. But no! You're nothing but an arrogant know-it-all, aren't you?"

"It's your fault." He shook his head. "If you would've gotten here sooner—"

"All right, you two," Sabrina said.

"Are you all right, Aribella?" Elliott asked.

"Yes, thanks to this young man."

Kristian gave Gracie a smirk. His sister shook her head.

"You saved my life," Aribella said.

He felt a bit strange. It was the first time he'd managed to get himself out of trouble without Gracie's help, and it felt good.

"What brings you here, Elliott?" Aribella asked.

"We're searching for King Malakon. He's disappeared."

"Are those two boys still at it?" she asked. "They've been going at each other forever. Are they still looking for that golden heart?"

Kristian's eye twitched as he glanced at Sirus. He leaned close to Aribella. "Do you know anything about a diamond box? Or, a key?"

She stared into his eyes. "Ruben lives in that mountain over there. I think I remember seeing a diamond box on a mantle in his room. It's been rumored that there's a key inside it."

Kristian's eyes widened.

"Why do you ask?"

He hobbled over and whispered in Elliott's ear; he needed to know if she could be trusted.

"With your life," the Friesian said.

Kristian took her aside and explained to her what he'd seen in the white book on Mighty Loft. Aribella lowered her head. A key dangled from a rope around her neck.

"Take this key. It unlocks Ruben's castle doors at the top of the mountain, but you'll need to enter the mountain from below because there may not be an entrance large enough for the Friesians to enter at the top of the castle. The Pippins will keep you safe, but I must warn you; don't touch their wall of green while they're spinning."

He nodded.

"And keep a careful eye out for the three heads." She dashed off like a gazelle and disappeared in the blizzard.

"Three heads?" Kristian called after her. "Wait, what are you talking about?"

THIRTEEN

A warm tropical breeze took the place of the blizzard, so Elliott and Sabrina were free to fly. They crested the mountain range. The air smelled fresh as they soared over a valley of palm trees, flowers, and a green blanket of vibrant flora. A massive waterfall poured down several plateaus, emptied over the side of the mountain, and plundered into a sea of nothingness off the edge of the planet. It was as if someone had sliced off part of the planet.

Hundreds of castle turrets protruded from the mountain's peak where a red beacon flashed in a circle from the highest turret.

"What's with the beacon?" Kristian asked Mikal.

"Ruben's third eye, I guess."

"You mean he knows we're here?" A woozy feeling squirmed around in his stomach.

"Not sure."

Gracie swiped her hair off her moist forehead. "It has to be a hundred degrees here."

They landed near the mountain's forbidding entrance, and they could see straight into the vast, infinite core. Green, glowing lights like lightning bugs floated throughout the cave. Kristian rubbed his stiff neck. It still ached from the fall.

"Sirus, we'd better tie your ears up, or they'll get stuck on something, and you'll hang yourself." Elliott snickered, and the donkey sneered. Kristian wrapped Sirus's ears a few times around his neck. He looked like he was wearing a turtleneck sweater. "Perfect," Kristian said.

Elliott and Sabrina crept into the mountain's entrance. As they made their way around some stalagmites, the veiled light hovered ahead near brown stalactites that hung upside down like dripping candles. Kristian flinched when he heard some hissing sounds. Farther ahead, a waterfall burst over a wall and emptied into an ebony lake. But the veiled light had vanished.

"I think we should go that way." Gracie pointed.

"I think we should go this way." Kristian nodded. Although his sister pointed in the direction of the veiled light, he couldn't give in to her opinion. Besides, his way looked more interesting.

"You're so stubborn." She scrunched her nose. He grinned without her knowledge. They crossed a stone bridge and strode deeper into the mountain's core.

"Did anyone hear that? It sounded like hissing sounds." Kristian peered through the cavern. They all shook their heads. A gust of wind pushed against them. The Friesians pranced against the gusts that carried earthy scents of wet decay. Kristian wrapped his arms around Sirus and gripped Elliott's mane.

"Now what, brains?" Gracie asked. No sooner did she get the words out than a gale force wind thrust her off Sabrina. She rolled off the edge of a cliff.

"Gracie!" He clung onto Elliott's mane and peered over the

edge of the cliff.

"I'm hanging on a ledge," she called out.

"I can't see you. Elliott, do something." Kristian peeked down into the darkness.

Elliott turned and rustled his tail down the side of the cliff while leaning into the wind. "Hurry!"

"Grab Elliott's tail," Kristian yelled down at Gracie.

"The wind's blowing it too hard. I can't reach it."

"Kristian, you'll need to slide down my tail so the weight of your body will keep my tail straight."

"Do be careful," Sabrina said.

Kristian grabbed Elliott's tail and closed his eyes as he slowly descended. He hoped he wouldn't fall and take Gracie with him.

"Faith," Sirus said.

The wind swept him back and forth until he felt Gracie's hand grab his foot.

"Okay." Her voice quivered. "Get me out of here." She wrapped her arms around Kristian's calves.

"Pull us up, Elliott."

Elliott moved forward until they were both safely up.

Kristian glanced at his sister. "Maybe we'll go the other way."

"Thank you," she said, cocky.

The wind gusts died down as they moved farther into the cave. Steam rose from the small lake surrounded by ferns, ivy, grasses, and shrubs. A small, narrow waterfall poured off a cliff. Above the waterfall, a giant bald eagle sat perched on a massive branch. Elliott's withers quivered. SanDorak lay stretched beside the lake, snoring. Around her thigh was a ragged, bloodstained bandage.

"We need to get up to Ruben's castle," Kristian said.

"Look." Sabrina jutted her snout.

A man paced below with his hands clasped behind him. He was tall and slender with slumped shoulders. Black knee boots covered black pants. He wore a sheath with a silver-handled sword tucked inside. Kristian barely saw a silver skeleton key swaying from a chain around his waist.

A short, hunched man scooted from behind the falls. Only his toes were visible beneath his tan robe.

"Who are they?" Kristian asked Mikal.

"Ruben and Melvin. Melvin was once a mighty warrior and led Ruben's army until he hurt his back."

Kristian sympathized with the poor man's injury.

The men's voices drifted through the cavern. "Melvin, I told you to have them followed."

Melvin hung his head the same way Meme had after Mikal had scolded her.

"That despicable brother of mine." Ruben turned. "I know he has the key to the golden heart. We must find the kid that Malakon was mumbling about."

Kristian's muscles stiffened.

Both men shuffled out of sight behind the waterfall.

Mikal peered at Kristian. "I wonder what kid he could be talking about."

"Let's just try to find Malakon." Kristian hoped Mikal didn't notice him swallow so hard. He had to get into the castle without Mikal.

Elliott flicked his head. "Look."

"You know Earthlings can't see in the dark." Sabrina swished her tail.

Kristian gasped. "But... I can see. It looks like a cage up there on that ledge."

"I see it, too," Gracie said.

"That's impossible," Mikal blurted. "How can you?"

"Quite odd," Elliott said. "Quite odd, indeed."

Sirus stepped on a pile of rocks, causing them to plunder and clap until they smacked onto the cavern floor. "Oops."

"Way to go." Elliott snarled and swept Sirus back up onto his back. "I knew you'd be nothing but trouble."

"Let's go check that cage out," Kristian said.

The horses galloped down the cavern, jumped into the air, and soared through the expanse of the mountain's core. Gracie's face looked as if it was Christmas morning and she had discovered tons of gifts piled beneath the tree. They soared through passageways until they reached the top of a cliff, where they halted.

SanDorak loomed before them, blocking their path. Ruben stood at the base of the creature's neck, peeking around her head.

"I take it you're here for my brother, the impostor." His voice was gruff, his laugh eerie.

Kristian shivered. The man reminded him of the man in the

painting hanging in the stairway of the castle on Mighty Loft.

"You're a jealous and angry old man," Mikal called, "and the greatest of all deceivers. Where's Malakon?"

"Everyone knows who the real deceiver is." Ruben tugged on SanDorak's reins. She had grown restless.

The cave rumbled. Elliott and Sabrina pricked their ears, and Sirus trembled. Kristian felt Gracie's hot breath on his neck. He spotted the veiled light above Ruben. Sirus looked up at him.

"I see it," Kristian whispered.

Ruben raised his sword. "Give me the heart, Mikal, and I'll give you my disgraceful brother."

"I don't have it."

"What do we do now?" Kristian asked as his temples thumped. He murmured in Sirus's ear, "Tell me he's not talking about my mom's golden heart."

His friend remained silent.

"We need to get to that cage and see if that's where he's keeping Malakon," Mikal said.

Elliott nodded. "Sabrina?"

"SanDorak's in our way. Besides, we can't just shoot straight up over her in such a confined space."

"We have to try," he whispered. "Just stretch your wings and thrust them downward with all your might."

Gracie stroked Sabrina's neck. "You can do it. I believe in you."

Elliott thrust his wings high and then downward so forcefully that it caused Sabrina to flounder, and her wings grazed against the cliffs. Mikal slid and dangled from her mane as she thrashed to get control.

"Sabrina!" Kristian watched in horror. "Elliott, help her!"

"Give me the heart," Ruben shouted.

Sabrina managed to make it to the cliff, but Ruben and SanDorak swooped down. Elliott descended and hovered above them as she got control of herself.

"Your sword," Sirus whispered, "Throw it at SanDorak and divert her actions."

"No way. I've never killed anything in my life."

"It's highly unlikely you will this time either."

Gracie shook her head. "Just do it. Sabrina's in trouble."

"Don't worry; you won't penetrate that beast's thick hide deep enough to cause any great harm," Sirus said. "But you can slow her down."

"But I—" Kristian's heart raced as his hands grew sweaty. He had no choice. He fumbled for his sword but paused.

"Oh, brother." Gracie grabbed his shoulder and stood, straining to keep her balance. She snatched the sword from his hand, swirled it above her head, and hurled it. The sword wobbled as it spun through the air.

The blade's tip caught SanDorak's shoulder, slicing her hide and drawing blood. She screamed like a vicious animal as she toppled through the chamber. The sword clanged against the rocks and plummeted to the ground.

"SanDorak," Ruben shouted as he fought to restrain her.

"That should hold her for a while," Sirus said.

Elliott rushed to Sabrina. He rubbed his chin across the top of her head. "You okay?"

She nodded. "I'll be fine."

They jumped into the air with one of Elliott's wings beneath one of hers and sped through the hazy green mountain, passing catacombs in the narrow passages. Just as Kristian was about to ask Mikal about the catacombs, Mikal answered as if he knew what Kristian was going to ask.

"Chamber of Sorrows."

"It smells like a hundred skunks." Gracie pulled her shirt over her nose. "So you've been here before?"

"No, I read about them in Dia's history books."

"Stop." Ruben dropped in behind them on top of a giant bird that looked like it had just escaped from the Chamber of Sorrows. Kristian's skin prickled. The bird's sparse feathers stuck from its grayish-pink body, and loose folds of skin hung from its boney carriage like a shar-pei. He couldn't imagine how the creature could fly.

"I'm not the bad guy," Ruben shouted. "Don't believe anything Mikal tells you."

FOURTEEN

Elliott turned sharp, tossing Kristian down his side. His fingers slid through Elliott's mane and landed on the oily-skinned creature with a thump, throwing the creature off balance and causing it to jerk from side to side. It bumbled through the mountain's passageways while he clung for his life.

He gagged. The bird smelled like month-old garbage on a hot day. He dug his fingernails into the creature's slimy skin, but he still slid, inch by inch, down the oily skin.

Ruben glared at him as he stretched his arm. "Grab my hand."

"So you can drop me?" Kristian grunted as he slid several more inches. He bounced up and down as if hanging from a bungee cord. The bird floundered down the chambers. Kristian stared at Ruben's outstretched hand—he was inches from salvation, seconds from grace.

"Confound it—grip my hand. I'm not who they say I am. I'm the real king of Dia. My brother's the impostor."

Kristian clung to the bird's oily skin by his fingertips. One hand slipped off. His face grew hot. Finally, he reached up and gripped Ruben's hand just as his other hand slipped. Ruben seized his wrist and jerked him up.

He trembled as he stared into the man's familiar amber eyes. His father had once told him the eyes were the entrance to people's hearts. Right now, Ruben's stare seemed to cause time to stand still, leaving Kristian feeling peaceful, but soon snapped out of it when the bird flapped haphazardly through the smoky mountain chambers.

"Who are you?" Ruben's voice was kind but anxious. "Why are you here with Mikal?"

Kristian hated telling half-truths, especially after promising Gracie he wouldn't, and he was trying to work on that, but—

"My father disappeared. I'm trying to find him." His stomach tightened into a clump like clay. He gasped when he noticed a mole beneath the man's ear.

"I lost my father, too. I think my brother may have... He knew that my father—" The bird floundered down another chamber. Ruben's eyes gleamed. "Might you know anything about a golden heart? I must find it before my brother does, but I haven't been able to find any clues, and he's not talking."

Kristian swallowed. "Why should I know anything about a golden heart?"

Ruben had a faraway expression on his face. "I believe the heart is the only thing that can save Dia. I overheard King Aaron talking about it. I must get back to Dia."

The bird tilted, throwing Kristian sideways. He almost slipped down the side, but he held tight. Out of nowhere, someone had jumped on Ruben and knocked him backward.

"Gracie, get off him." Kristian clung to the bird's loose skin and couldn't get any traction to free her arms from around Ruben's neck. He dug his fingernails into the bird's leathery hide to keep from falling. She clung tight to Ruben's neck as her legs thrashed about. Her braids whipped like reddish-blond snakes.

Ruben clung to the bird with one hand and tugged Gracie's arms with his other. "Get off me."

"You stay away from my brother." She grunted as she clamped her legs around Ruben's waist, hanging on him like a monkey on its mother's neck.

"Your brother," Ruben shouted.

"That's right. And it's a good thing I jumped when I did." She glared at Kristian. "I always have to save your butt."

"I was doing just fine without you," Kristian snapped. But he didn't want to think about what he'd do without her.

Ruben twisted and finally popped Gracie's legs loose from around his waist. Kristian struggled toward the bird's neck. He managed to reach out and press firmly on its neck.

"Down," he told the creature calmly, and it soared downward. Elliott swooped in with Sirus and grabbed the bird's scrawny neck. "No, I have it under control."

Elliott let go. The bird plunged to a nearby ledge, throwing Kristian, Gracie, and Ruben. Sabrina soared toward them with Mikal. He dropped down before her hooves hit the ground, rushed over, and got in Ruben's face. He gritted his teeth and pounced, pinning Ruben's arms behind his back.

"You won't get away with it this time."

Ruben's muscles bulged beneath his sleeves as he whirled his attacker around, locking his arms behind his back. He flipped Mikal to the ground and held him.

Mikal's eyes bulged as he squirmed to escape. "I'll get you."

Ruben scrambled back on the bird and disappeared into the smoke. The mountain rumbled, sending loose rocks plundering. Kristian spotted the veiled light as it drifted toward the mountain's entrance. It waved up and down several times as if it were trying to tell him something.

"I think we need to leave," Sirus said.

"But I have to find the box." His stomach tightened as he glanced across the chasm. "Look. It's a stairway leading to Ruben's castle. We can go that way."

"Suit yourself." The little donkey shook his head in slow motion.

This time an eagle swooped down carrying Ruben, who jumped off and pulled his sword. Mikal stumbled backward and slammed into the wall.

"The only way…you're taking my brother out of here…is tied up on your vessel with me." Ruben heaved in and out. He grasped the children's arms and ushered them into a steel cage in a nearby alcove. He clicked the locked. The cage was bigger than the one Malakon occupied. "I'm doing this for your own good.
You'll be safe here. I'll be back."

He scrambled back up on his eagle and dashed off. Kristian clutched his stomach. Fear forced his heart to quiver. He kicked sand and smacked his foot against the steel bars.

"He won't be back," Mikal sneered.

"Get us out of here," Kristian said.

But Mikal turned and stood with his hands on his hips, looking over the edge of the cliff.

"Mikal!" Kristian grabbed the bars. The mountain trembled. Rocks clattered against the walls and plunged down through the chasm. He stared through blurry eyes at the veiled light as it hovered near the entrance to the cave. When he looked closer this time, he saw a tiny flame flicker beneath the veil. He gripped the warm bars. "Help us!"

"Who're you yelling at?" Gracie squinted. "We wouldn't be in this mess if it weren't for you."

"If you're so smart then get us out of here." That should make her feel guilty.

Her face turned deep pink. "I'm getting tired of helping you all the time."

His heart pounded. *Oh, she can't give up on me now.*

"Then don't help. Who needs you?" He trembled as he gripped the cage bars, kicking sand through the bars as if kicking it at the veiled light.

"For the last time, who are you talking to?" Gracie asked. "Mikal's not paying attention to you."

Kristian ignored her and continued calling out to the veiled light. "I'm tired of you showing up, never speaking, and never helping." He pounded the bars. A sharp pain stabbed his palms. Sweat dribbled down his temple. He bent over and gasped as he clung to the bars. "Either do something or leave me alone!"

Gracie placed her hand on his back. "Slow, deep breaths."

After he calmed down, he glanced back at the veiled light. It was gone.

"No! Come back." He crumpled to his knees. "I didn't mean it. I didn't mean to say—" He shivered. A cold, lonely feeling swept through him as he stared across the smoky chasm. "Now, what have I done?" he muttered.

"What's wrong with you?" Gracie touched his shoulder.

He knocked her hand off. "Just leave me alone."

Smoke filtered through the bars. They tugged their shirts over their noses and shouted for help. She clutched the bars. "Look. There's Sabrina, Elliott, and Sirus."

The trio landed. "We've been looking all over for you two. Stand back." Sabrina kicked at the lock, but it held fast. She tried again. No luck. "Elliott, you try."

He kicked. It didn't break.

"Okay, start digging beneath the bars on that side, and we'll do the same on this side," Sabrina said.

Kristian and Gracie dropped to their knees and flung sand between their legs while Elliott and Sabrina pawed their hooves to remove the sand from beneath the bars. When the hole was large enough, the children squeezed through and scrambled out.

"Let's go." Mikal scrambled up on Sabrina.

"Oh, now you decide to talk," Kristian yelled.

They raced across the smoky chasm. Kristian thought his heart would burst when he spotted the veiled light again. It had returned. It acted as though it wanted them to follow it out of the mountain.

Kristian glanced at Sirus, who was glaring at him. "But I have to find the box. If we can just get to the castle and get the box, we can get out of this place."

"Suit yourself, but I don't think that's a good idea."

He had to try it if he had any chance of finding it.

Sirus shivered against him. "I must say, something doesn't feel right—"

Kristian gripped Elliott's mane and kicked his flanks. "Get us to the castle fast."

Sabrina flew parallel above them. "I don't think—"

Gracie flung her arms around his waist as Elliott raced up through the chasm. As they got closer, he saw faded lights through the castle's portals on the side of the mountain.

"I can't do this," Elliott scolded. "We must get out of here." A boulder just missed them.

"Wait." His heart pumped faster. "Drop me on that ledge. I'll go myself."

"You can't," Gracie shouted.

Elliott landed on a cliff near a wooden bridge that stretched across the chasm. The ledge on the other side leading to the castle seemed too narrow for Elliott.

"Sirus, come with me," Kristian said.

"I don't think...I should probably not..." Sirus ambled toward him.

"Are you sure you won't come?" Kristian glanced at the Friesians. He swallowed hard, waiting for them to comply.

"We can't let them go by themselves," Sabrina said.

Mikal slid off. "I'm not going."

Kristian was relieved about that.

Elliott shook his head and glanced at Sabrina, and then at the children. "I'm sorry, but it's not safe for us. We'll need to wait here."

"Well, then, we can at least search for the king," Sabrina sighed.

Kristian, Gracie, and Sirus plodded to the rope bridge. "I don't do rope bridges," Sirus said, "with my short legs and all."

"Then I'll carry you." Kristian grunted as he pushed and prodded Sirus until he'd situated him on his shoulders. He wrapped Sirus's wiggling legs around his neck, as a shepherd would carry a lamb.

Sirus grunted.

He grasped Sirus's hooves in one hand, gripped the rope rail with the other, and stepped onto the flimsy, wobbly bridge. Sirus's belly felt warm against his neck, but Kristian still shivered. He slid his hand across the prickly rope, inch by inch, and tottered across the wooden slats.

Gracie was already halfway across the bridge. "Come on, you guys."

Sirus's teeth clattered. "Don't…l-l-look…d-down."

"Talking to yourself again?" Kristian didn't dare tell him that he was terrified of heights too.

"You scared?" Sirus asked. "You're shaking more than me."

"Uh oh. We have a situation up here." Gracie stopped. The

bridge jerked and swayed. "And it's coming our way."

She turned and jutted back across the wooden slats toward Kristian and Sirus. Kristian could barely see past Sirus's tail. His jaw tightened. "What's wrong?"

"It's the mother of all nightmares—run!" She clomped back across the bridge causing it to jiggle more. "They're scorpions! And s-spiders—rat-sized, and hundreds of them!"

"Stop rocking the bridge." There was one other thing they had in common—hating spiders.

"Ouch!" Her foot scraped the back of his heel. His palms burned as he slid them across the rope. "We'll be stung and bitten alive."

The mountain quaked. A giant boulder streaked through the chasm and slammed into the footbridge, slicing it in half. Kristian grabbed the ropes. Sirus clung to his neck. Gracie dove toward him and clutched his pant pockets just in time. All three slammed against the wall as the scorpions and spiders plunged into the smoky abyss.

"Sirus, climb over me and get to the ledge. My hands are slipping."

The donkey grunted as he prodded up and over Kristian's head until he scrambled onto the ledge. Kristian helped Gracie, and they all made it to safety. There was another bridge—this one made of stone—several yards away. He hadn't seen it earlier. They stumbled across the bridge to the other side, as flames hurled up around them. They trudged up the stone stairs, and stopped in front of a huge, black iron door.

He slipped the key Aribella gave him into the lock, turned it with a click, and nudged the door open. They crept down a dim hall with a vaulted ceiling that looked like fish ribs. Several tall, rectangular, stained-glass windows bowed up the sides of the wall to the ceiling. Kristian searched for a semicircular, vaulted room with a wooden desk, the one he'd seen in the white book. At the end of the hall, he spotted a portrait of a king and queen above the marble ledge of a fireless fireplace.

Cool, stale air brushed past them as they moved farther along. On the left was a large dining hall with rectangular, antique tables, a candelabras atop each one. On the right was a gloomy library filled with old, dusty books. They reached an open staircase with one armored knight standing on each side, each one holding a copper plate with a small torch flickering atop each plate.

The children climbed the stairs while Sirus waited. Gracie clung to Kristian's shirt as they crept down a long, chilly hall. A spider web caressed Kristian's face, and he stumbled as he fought to remove it.

A streak of light sprayed across the burnt orange carpet at the end of the hall, and a tangy odor drifted past. When the floor squeaked, he halted. Gracie bumped into him, and he gave her an annoyed glance.

He leaned over and peeked inside the dimly lit room. "Look," he said, barely above a whisper. "It's the box."

Gracie lost her balance. She would've toppled on the floor if he hadn't reached out and grabbed her. He shook his head as he gave her a disgusting sigh.

A tall man stood by a large bay window with his back toward

them. Kristian froze, staring at the box. He hustled toward it, snatched it from its mantle, and whizzed past Gracie. "Come on."

"Stop," the man called.

Heavy thuds followed them down the hall as their feet pounded the carpet.

"It's Ruben," Gracie yelled. They flailed down the steps two at a time, and his clubfoot ached. They caught up with Sirus, and all three bolted from the castle, dodging chucks of falling debris as they raced back across the bridge. On the other side, they scrambled up on top of Elliott.

"Go," Kristian yelled, as the Friesians glided through the cavern. "Did you find the king?"

"No," Sabrina answered.

Kristian felt Sirus trembling against his chest.

FIFTEEN

"What's wrong?" Kristian followed Sirus's horrified gaze. His eyes were as big as walnuts. Six, ruby red eyes glared down at them, and they were connected to the biggest, blackest, three-headed snake this side of the universe.

Elliott and Sabrina landed and slid to a halt. The snake coiled. It had to be the 'three heads' Aribella had warned them about.

Gracie screamed and jabbed Kristian's shoulders. "T-That's the beast that tried to snatch me from the meadows."

He couldn't swallow. "I know."

The serpent slithered toward them. It jabbed its forked tongues in and out. Hundreds of wings stretched across the creature's back, buzzing like a swarm of bees. Sabrina jutted toward the creature.

"No," Elliott called.

Gracie shook Kristian. "Pull your sword."

"You threw it at SanDorak!"

The snake slithered toward them, moving its heads up and down like dancing gypsies move their arms.

"Just get us out of here," Mikal shouted at Sabrina.

"I will not leave them."

"There's your sword." Gracie pointed. Kristian glanced down and saw the sword sticking from a pile of rubble.

Sabrina batted her wings at the creature. "Hurry. Grab it."

He slid off as Elliott raced around the other side and batted his wings at the creature. Kristian dropped the box as he stumbled toward the pile of rubble. He stared at the sword.

One of the serpent's heads slithered toward Sabrina. Another of the creature's heads slithered toward him. She turned and slammed her hind hooves between the snake's eyes. The snake's head snapped backward, but the creature caught her with one of its other heads and hurled her through the cavern. She hit the wall and faltered to the ground.

"Sabrina!"

"Over here, you creep." Gracie jumped up and down, batting her arms in all directions. One of the snake's heads slithered toward her and Sirus. It hissed. It coiled. Its necks looked like fishhooks, and its head bolted toward them.

Kristian planted his feet and yanked his sword out. He stood eye-to-eye with the creature. "Believe. Believe. Believe," he murmured through clenched teeth. His fingers began to turn numb. He grunted and swished the sword through the air. One of the creature's heads dropped with a thud. He had hit it. He felt woozy. The smell of blood and stench swirled about him.

Gracie and Sirus screamed as another head lowered itself in front of them. Its icy breath blew over them. It smelled decayed wood. Its forked, black tongue slid in and out between crusty, wrinkled lips. It jutted its head and gripped them both in its mouth.

Sirus squirmed. Gracie screamed. Kristian inched his quivering hand into his pocket, gripping the heart and shoving it in the air.

The serpent shrieked and jerked. It whipped its remaining two heads in all directions until Gracie and Sirus dropped. Sabrina swooped in before they hit the ground and snatched them.

"Press the emerald crystal inside the pommel of the sword," Ruben echoed through the chamber. He was now riding the eagle, sword drawn. The snake turned a head toward Ruben. "The pommel!"

Kristian slid his thumb onto the bumpy surface and pressed. The sword's blade glowed red, and a laser shot from its tip. He gripped the handle in both hands. The blade sliced through the air making zapping sounds.

The snake's tail slapped the cave walls as it screamed and squirmed. Kristian sliced the laser through the air. The snake's head slammed to the ground with a deafening thud.

"Look out," Gracie shouted.

The last head plucked Kristian off the ground and shook him senseless. The laser zigzagged through the cavern. The eagle dove and dug its talons into the serpent's neck, spraying blood, while Ruben stayed behind on the cliff.

With a loud thud, Kristian crashed to the ground in the creature's mouth. The snake's head jerked and wailed. He scrambled out and crawled toward a large pile of rubble. Ruben sat on his Friesian stallion, holding his sword streaked with blood.

"I've had enough of this," Gracie shouted.

Kristian glanced at his sister. It was the worse he'd seen her. Her hair stuck out like porcupine quills, and her face looked smudged with something that looked like soot. The mountain rumbled. He'd had enough too. "Let's go."

The bedrock cracked, hurling heat up through it. Elliott and Sabrina jumped into the air just before the ground split. Rocks had blocked the entrance, so they turned and ascended toward the mountaintop.

"The veiled light tried to warn you." Sirus's voice quivered.

"Look out," Sabrina screamed.

The next thing Kristian heard was a thump. Then Elliott's neck wrenched and went limp. Then his wings did the same. He spiraled toward the ground while Kristian, Gracie, and Sirus leaned backward and clung to his mane for their lives.

"Elliott!" Kristian tugged on his mane. "Wake up!"

Sabrina swooped down and barely broke Elliott's fall before hitting the ground with a heart-wrenching thud as if all the air left Elliott's lungs and rushed out his mouth. Kristian, Gracie, and Sirus tumbled over each other and rolled to a stop.

Kristian shook the fuzziness from his head and hobbled to Elliott.

Sabrina licked Elliott's gaping wound. "Don't you dare leave me."

"Please, get up." Kristian laid his head against Elliott's chest. He felt he'd die if anything happened to his friend. "He's barely breathing." Kristian's heart sank. Why hadn't he listened to Sirus? Why did he always have to be a stubborn know-it-all like Gracie said?

"I knew we should've left." Gracie stroked Elliott's nose.

Kristian felt her icy stare.

"Get away," Kristian shouted.

"You don't care about anybody but yourself," she said, stomping her foot. "You're the most stubborn person I've ever known. Elliott told you he thought we should get out of here. Now look what you've done."

"Just leave me alone." He gritted his teeth.

"You didn't come here to find the king. You came here for your own selfish reasons, whatever they are."

At that moment, it was as though time stood still. He buried his head in his hands. Then he strolled several yards away from the group. Seeing Elliott lying there like that felt as if someone had ripped his heart out.

The mountain trembled.

He hobbled back to them and slid his hand down Elliott's neck. He had accepted him for whom he was—bad temper, bad attitude, bad foot, and all. "Please don't die. You can't die. Sabrina, you have to help him."

"Friesians are brave and strong." She spread her wings over all of them as debris fell. Warm drops dripped on Kristian's head. "We try to prepare for such things, but sometimes there is nothing that can be done. You risked his life. I almost want to not forgive you."

Kristian's world went black. He'd let everyone down. He gripped his stomach and buried his face in Elliott's neck. Warmth rushed over him.

"We can't move him, and Sabrina can't lift him," Gracie said.

She stepped back, shaking her head.

He jumped to his feet. "Well, we're not going to leave him here."

"The Dians' fate lies in your hands," Sirus said. "Listen to your heart."

"I have no idea what its saying. I don't hear anything. I never do." But maybe he did. He thought about the veiled light. Maybe his heart and the veiled light were connected somehow.

"Or is it that you choose to ignore it?" Sirus said.

A giant, green blur swooped down through the mountain's chamber.

"Look, it's the Pippins," Gracie shouted, jumping up and down. "They've come to help."

The tiny birds swirled around them in a glorious array of twinkling green lights.

"It's about time," Sabrina said with a smile and sighed. "I thought you'd never get here."

Kristian, Gracie, and Sirus rushed toward Elliott and knelt. The Pippins formed a swirling wall around them as rocks crashed to the ground. Kristian became so mesmerized with their spinning wall that he inched his finger toward them without thinking.

"No," Sabrina shouted.

But it was too late. He lost his balance and jerked his finger into the green, swirling wall. Bright, green lights flashed every-which-way, popping like firecrackers. The Pippins shrieked and screamed as they zigged and zagged and swished. The pathetic sound pierced his heart. Their delicate bodies flicked and flittered as they bounced off the cave walls like rubber balls until finally yielding to their dilemma on the bedrock. He gawked as he stared at their lifeless, green bodies.

"Now look what you did," Mikal snarled.

"You just don't—" Gracie let out a deep moan. "Aribella told you not to touch them when they were spinning. How would anyone think you could save Dia?"

His throat tightened as if someone hit him in his Adam's apple. He glanced at the tiny, unmoving bodies scattered across the bedrock, fell to his knees, and stared absently through the mountain chamber, straining to see if he could spot the veiled light. "Please, if you're out there, please help my friend, Elliott. Take me instead."

The mountain rumbled.

"Who're you talking to?" Mikal shuffled up behind him.

"Leave him alone." Sirus sat next to Kristian. "Faith takes root in the heart. If you would only—"

As if on cue, the rocks stopped falling.

"I didn't mean what I said." Kristian clutched his head. He stared all around looking for the veiled light and then looked at Sirus. "This is all my fault."

The little donkey remained silent as the mountain rumbled and the cavern floor grew hotter.

Kristian gathered the still bodies in his arms and placed them delicately in a crumpled heap. He slid his finger across one of the tiny, green bodies. "Meme will never forgive me. We should've left."

"Don't rehash the past," Sirus said. "Go forth now and learn from it."

A warm gust of wind swirled through the mountain's core. Meme slid to a halt in front of Kristian's face and stared into his eyes. With drooping shoulders, she flitted over to the green heap and placed her wing over her breast. She gently shook her head. "My poor, dear Pippins."

She fluttered back to him. He inched his limp arm to salute her, the same way she did to him when they first met on the *Cosmic Star*, but she didn't salute back. His lips quivered. "I-I-I'm so...sor—"

"You touched the wall." Meme placed the back of her hand on her forehead.

He nodded.

"These tiny creatures are so delicate that if you touch the wall when they're spinning, it throws them off balance."

"I didn't mean to, really, I just—" He lowered his head.

"You're still not listening?"

"Yes. No. I don't know. What am I supposed to be hearing?" He turned his back to her. He couldn't bear to look into her pitiful eyes.

She fluttered around him to the other side. With the tip of her wing, she reached under his chin and slowly lifted until she looked him square in the eye. "I'm glad I met you, Kristian."

He remembered telling her the same when they met.

"I'm glad to call you my friend. If you are to finish your journey victoriously, you must dig deep inside yourself and find the faith that will lead you to victory."

"But, I don't know how."

"You must obey as well as listen, but above all, you must learn to trust that still, small voice because it cares for you. Someone created this universe and everything in it. And that someone loves and cares deeply for you. But you must believe. Let the voice guide you, and you won't be disappointed." She glanced at the Pippins. "They have only been dazed. We'll know in a minute if they'll be okay."

His eyes widened as the seconds turned to minutes. Meme fluttered over to the Pippins. She stopped, swirled around them, and sprinkled them with gold glitter.

"Come, dear ones, arise."

Groggy, they stirred from their heap.

"Are they going to be okay?"

"I believe they will be. We'll meet you back on the *Cosmic Star*." Meme zipped off, and the Pippins groggily followed.

It felt as though someone had breathed new life into him—a second chance. What relief. He looked around for the veiled light.

"Please, I'll do better—listening, I mean. Please, help Elliott." He held his breath as he glanced around. "I believe."

The whisper barely swept past his lips. But he'd said it.

"I—choose—to—believe." This time he said it louder. As soon as the words left his mouth, something unexplainable happened deep within him, as if someone was speaking to his heart.

Sirus whispered, "All things are possible to those who believe. Hope follows belief."

"I do believe." A warm sensation rolled over his skin. Kristian closed his eyes and took a deep breath. When he opened them, he looked around, and there, in the darkness, he spotted the veiled light. It had taken the shape of a tiny, golden heart shining beneath the veil.

Sabrina whinnied. Ruben disappeared up through the chasm on his Friesian, while the bald eagle descended, landed near Elliott, and folded its wings to its sides. Its white and tan feathers glistened, and it clicked its talons across the bedrock and stood in front of Sabrina. Sabrina nodded. She spread her wings and bowed.

Gracie didn't blink.

The eagle wrapped one set of wings around Elliott, cradled him to its breast, and lifted his limp body. With the other set of wings, it flew swiftly out of the mountain.

Kristian hobbled after them and stopped. "No, bring him back."

Sabrina smiled and touched his shoulder with the tip of her wing. "The creature is delivering him to the vessel. I believe Elliott will be all right."

"Really?" He sighed and hugged her neck. His heart warmed.

"Faith doesn't always guarantee that things will turn out the way we want," Sirus said, "but faith is known for moving mountains and for overcoming the world in ways we sometimes can't understand."

Then as if the planet woke from its slumber, the mountain shook, and rocks plundered in large chunks, smacking the cave walls before smashing to pieces on the ground.

"We have to get out of here, now!" Kristian shouted.

SIXTEEN

When Kristian and the others reached the *Cosmic Star*, Elliott had recovered from his ordeal. Kristian threw his arms around his neck. "I'm so glad you're okay."

Elliott smiled. "Me too. Where's the king?"

Kristian clutched his mouth and gasped. "Oh, no, the king. Sabrina—"

"Hop up," Elliott said. "I'll take you."

"You're in no condition to—" Sabrina began.

"I'm okay, *Mom*." They raced back to the mountain through streaks of fire that spewed from the top. He shot through the cavern and up to the ledge. His hooves barely touched the ground when Kristian slid down, flung himself onto the ground, and rushed to the cage. He swung open the door. A man lay slumped against the black bars, moaning. Elliott stretched his neck in and slid him out.

Kristian's eyes widened. The man looked identical to Ruben.

"It's Malakon."

"Wait until I get my hands on my brother." Malakon's voice was gruff and weak as he glared at Kristian. "Who are you?" But he passed out before Kristian could answer.

"Let's get him back." Kristian held the stranger in his arms until they reached the *Cosmic Star*. By now, Mikal was maneuvering the vessel towards the wormhole. He glanced back at the planet and wondered why it had succumbed to such upheaval. It was near imploding.

Gracie jumped up and down at the aft and waved her arms like a crazed gorilla.

The mountaintop exploded. Trapped gases burst high in the air. Yellow lava overflowed and oozed down its sides. The stinging sulfuric acid drifted across the sky in smoky plumes, as the mountain spit fireballs. Just before Elliott neared the vessel, a shockwave ripped across the planet and propelled him toward the ship like a shooting star. He flicked and flailed.

"Control your wings before we crash."

Another shockwave hurled across the planet as they neared the *Cosmic Star*. Just as it entered the wormhole the shock hurled Elliott across the main deck. The jolt tossed Kristian and Malakon through the air. They toppled over each other and bumped into the base of a mast, jerking them to a halt. The king's face looked pallid, and his eyes looked like two danish rolls with blueberry centers.

"Get off me," the king demanded.

Kristian helped him up. "Are you all right, sir? I mean, your Highness. I mean—"

"I'm fine...just fine." He grimaced, tugged his arm away, and brushed himself off with trembling fingers. He sounded like an old, finicky hermit. How was Kristian to know how to talk or act around a king?

Gracie curtsied and acted all giddy, as if she had just met her favorite movie star. She was only trying to show him up. Kristian shook his head. The king wobbled toward Mikal at the helm. Kristian crept behind him, hoping he could snatch some of their conversation.

"What took you so long?" Malakon grumbled in a loud whisper.

Mikal glanced down. "Your Highness, I—"

"Never mind." Malakon waved his hand. "It doesn't matter."

Mikal glanced at Kristian, who turned and pretended he wasn't paying attention. Mikal reached for his king's hand, and when he bent down to kiss it the king jerked his hand away.

"Stop fussing over me." The king sneered. "What happened to my brother, anyway?"

"I don't think he escaped the planet, your Highness." Mikal acted submissive and meek, which told Kristian he wasn't the hot shot he pretended to be. He flicked his eyes at Kristian.

A large, white feather swooped across the deck and landed behind a wooden bucket on the poop deck. He turned toward the stern but couldn't tell where it came from.

The king strolled up. "Who are you, lad?"

"Kristian…MacNeal, your Highness." He stepped back and stared at the mole beneath the king's left ear.

"We'll talk later. For now, take the wheel." Malakon rubbed his chin as he glared at Kristian's mole. He glanced at Mikal. "Come along."

Mikal jumped down and glowered at Kristian. He reached for the king's arm, but he jerked it away. They trod down some steps and disappeared below the poop deck.

"I'm glad you made it," Gracie said.

Kristian lifted the corner of his mouth and grinned. Why couldn't she be nice all the time?

Sabrina plopped Sirus on top of the crate next to Kristian at the helm.

"I thought it'd be awesome to meet a king," Kristian said, "but he's nothing but a grumpy, old man. And he's been acting terribly suspicious." He slipped Ruben's small box from his pocket and turned it over. He grimaced at the keyhole. "Seriously? Not another keyhole with no key."

Sirus cleared his throat and grinned.

"What's so funny?" He glanced at him and saw a tiny, silver skeleton key sticking from the side of his hairy mouth.

"Are you kidding me? Where'd you get it?" Kristian slipped the key from the donkey's lips.

"When the eagle flew down to get Elliott, it flipped me the key."

"But why? And why did he give it to you?" Footsteps forced him to stuff the box and the key into his pocket.

"I'll take over now," Mikal said.

Malakon stood on the second deck, peering at the swirling particles rotating around the vessel. He looked pale. Gracie came up from the galley carrying a basket filled with fruit and bread. When they finished eating, Kristian and Sirus found a comfortable spot against the hull.

"We animals have a bond between us and a keen sense," Sirus said in answer to Kristian's questions. "The eagle is no different. It sensed that you needed the key."

He rested his head on Kristian's lap, and they drifted off to sleep to the rocking and creaking of the vessel.

SEVENTEEN

Gracie jiggled Kristian's shoulder. "Why's it so dark?"

He rubbed his eyes and focused. "What's wrong? It's only been a few minutes, why'd you wake me up?"

"A few minutes? You and Sirus have been asleep for at least half an hour."

"Not to worry." Sirus lifted his head. He made a sucking sound. "We're just going through the core."

Kristian closed his eyes. He couldn't sleep. His foot throbbed, reminding him of his purpose for being here: to find the secret of his mom's golden heart so hopefully it might have the power to heal his foot, and to find his dad, and who knew what else? But he wasn't expecting to inherit his mom's destiny, whatever that was. And how had she gotten the heart?

He opened his eyes. Darkness still surrounded them. Sirus moved his head on Kristian's lap. Kristian scratched Sirus's neck and wondered what happened to the kings, Aaron and Ramón. How could they just disappear? Had Ruben been right—that Malakon was behind his and Gracie's father's disappearance? Both brothers claimed to be heirs to his throne. How could he tell who was lying and who was telling the truth? Gracie might know, since she was pretty good at spotting liars.

The throbbing in his foot faded. Did being normal really depend upon a person's physical body, or did it have to do with a person's heart, and how they acted or the choices they made? His clubfoot was part of who he was whatever the reason.

Kristian snapped out of his daze when the vessel jolted and lurched out the other side of the wormhole. They headed down the Cosmic River toward Dia. His stomach quivered when he thought about seeing Linnea.

Sabrina applied more salve to Elliott's wound. The twins stood at the hull and allowed the cold breeze to blow across their faces as they stared into the universe. It reminded him of the nights he and his dad camped on the cliffs of Lake Superior, falling asleep to chirping crickets and hoot owls.

Gracie sighed. "Who will believe us when we tell them about all of this?"

"Only those who choose to believe in something bigger than themselves, even when they don't understand any of it." Kristian grinned at Sirus.

"I wish Mom and Dad were here." Her tone grew weary, and her eyes glimmered from the lights of the cosmos.

Meme pricked Kristian's shoulder, and he winced. Gracie chuckled, bringing her out of her slump.

"Ta, ta. The Pippins are ready for their treat now. It's been a long journey." The little pixie nodded.

Kristian turned and saw the Pippins lined in several rows like soldiers at boot camp, scratching their tiny claws across the deck while pricking their mouse-sized ears forward.

Gracie chuckled louder. "Go on."

"I'm glad you find this funny."

Meme nodded. "Treats are in that bag over there. Ta, ta. You don't want to see them when they're really hungry."

Everyone chuckled as Kristian opened the bag. He jerked his head back and made a horrid groan. The strong cheesy odor blasted him in the face. "Gross."

Kristian tugged his shirt over his nose and scooped the gooey lumps out and dolloped them onto the deck. Half the goo remained on his hand.

The Pippins stampeded across the deck toward the first heap. They slurped and gobbled it up within minutes as their tiny beaks pecked the deck to get every drop. When they finished, they smacked their beaks, tweeted, and fluttered back to the masts. Kristian sighed deeply and saluted Meme, who straightened her pencil-thin body and flittered her wings as if someone had breathed new life into her. She saluted back and winked.

"You're the only one who's ever saluted me, sir." Her smile was as radiant as a moonbeam. She hummed as she dolloped to take her place among the Pippins, and soon they fell fast asleep.

Kristian hobbled down the deck and found a bucket of water to rinse off his hands. He slipped the heart from his pocket and stared at its flawless, shiny beauty.

Gracie gasped. He jerked around and shoved the heart back into his pocket. He stood stiff hoping she hadn't seen it.

"I saw it."

He let out a deep sigh and moaned as he stared at her while she held her hand over her mouth. Now the whole world would know he had his mom's heart.

"That's Mom's—" Kristian pulled her away from the others. She mumbled behind her hand, "You mean you had it all along, and you said nothing?"

"Quiet, will you?" He swiveled his head from side to side to see if anyone was listening.

"You said you didn't have it. You told Mom—"

"I know, I know. You can't tell anyone...please. Promise?" He knew he had to get her to promise, or she would slip and tell someone and then call it accidental. He knew that the one thing she always did was keep promises.

"Okay, okay. I promise." She stomped her foot. "Why didn't you tell Mom?"

"Because. The only one who knows is Sirus."

"Do you have the key, too?" He shook his head. "You know Mom's going to be furious."

"Don't look now, but the king's staring at us. We'll talk later." He put his finger horizontally to his lips.

Why was he staring at them so suspiciously? Why did he think a kid could save Dia? And from what? There was something about it that Kristian couldn't figure out, something really strange. Malakon just didn't act like a king.

But how would Kristian know how a king acts? He'd never met

one before.

***

The *Cosmic Star* squeaked against the pier at the edge of Dia. Grey clouds bloated the sky, swallowing the mountaintops. The planet had grown darker since they'd left. Flocks of bluebirds soared overhead. The Pippins flitted from the ship's masts and joined the bluebirds. A large crowd had gathered to greet them. Kristian searched for Linnea, but he didn't see her.

"Darkness always comes before the storm," Elliott whispered. "While Dia grows darker, we grow weaker." His head drooped as he clip-clopped down the deck.

"I'm feeling weaker myself," Kristian said to Sabrina.

"Well, you have been through a lot."

"Yeah, but this feels weird, like all my muscles are weak."

Mikal and Malakon stood at the hull and glared at the crowd.

Kristian got a sense there was some deep, dark secret among the people, and he decided that he was going to find what the underlying cause of it was or die trying. Someone or something seemed control them.

His dad had taught him and Gracie that the only real way to solve a problem was to get to the root of it because all the minor issues grew outward from the root. "If you can find the root," his dad had said, "then you'll be able to solve the problem and the smaller troubles will vanish."

This thought made him determined to find the root cause: why was the planet losing its light?

Malakon raised his hand to silence the crowd's murmurs. "Thank you for gathering here to welcome me back. As you can see, I'm safe."

Gracie leaned in to Kristian's ear. "They don't look very happy to see him."

"They look like zombies."

"Mikal risked his life to rescue me," the king continued. Mikal jutted his chin and smirked, giving Kristian a sly glance over his shoulder. The crowd gasped.

"But he didn't rescue him," Gracie murmured, "you did."

"Why would he lie like that?" Kristian couldn't know what the king was up to. "Why does everyone look like they're marching off to the guillotine?"

"But the great news is," the king continued, "you'll no longer need to worry about Ruben. He won't be coming back."

With that, the crowd broke up, and the Dians scattered. They looked like downtrodden, pathetic souls with hunched shoulders and heads bowed low.

"They're afraid of something," Kristian said. "But what?"

EIGHTEEN

Kristian found Linnea plucking faded flowers in the withered garden near the castle and heaving them into a pile. He watched as Gracie walked up to her. After exchanging words, Gracie ran over to him.

"She's really weird. She's so dainty and ladylike. It can make someone like me a little nauseous. Women need to be strong; after all, we're just as strong as men are. Anyway, come on, she's offered to fix us something to eat and a place to rest."

"Not every girl's a tomboy, you know. Some girls just like being a girl. What's wrong with that? Besides, you aren't— Never mind."

Gracie shrugged his remark away, and they followed Linnea inside Mighty Loft to a grand kitchen where cherry cabinets were mounted on pure white walls. Kristian gazed around the massive room. A shiny chrome stove sat inside a white brick alcove. Logs crackled and snapped in a fieldstone fireplace across the room.

They sat at a long table with a stained glass tabletop and shiny brass legs with royal blue velvet seat cushions.

Linnea moved with grace, clattering dishes as she prepared food. "Since King Aaron disappeared, the servants have not been to work."

Kristian watched her, but Gracie swatted his arm. "Stop staring."

He figured his sister probably knew he liked Linnea, being she was his twin and all. Linnea's shimmering, thick hair hung to her waist and swung softly as she moved. Her eyes were a striking blue like the ocean. Kristian couldn't find anything wrong with her.

"The Dians farm the land to the south." Linnea set a dish on the table that overflowed with sliced kiwi, apples, blueberries, peaches, and strawberries. Next, she set a bowl of steamed broccoli, carrots, peas, and lima beans down. Kristian scoop up the vegetables and carefully inched the lima beans to one side away from the other vegetables.

Gracie shook her head and gave a soft *tsk*.

"Why are the Dians hiding?" he asked. "And why do they look so pitifully sad?"

"Lima beans are good for your heart, you know." Linnea scooped more onto his plate, and his face turned warm.

She placed an oblong, tulip-designed platter on the table heaping with fish and chicken. The aroma made him a little lightheaded. It smelled just as good as when his mom cooked. He shoved the food into his mouth as if he was in an eating contest.
Again, Gracie nudged him under the table with her foot.

He waited for Linnea to answer his question.

She seemed comfortable in the kitchen cooking. His sister would rather be out hunting the food than be in the kitchen fixing it.

Everything was so tasty. Kristian even ate the lima beans, which to his surprise, tasted almost good. With his mouth full, he asked again, "Why are they hiding?"

"They trust no one anymore. And I must admit, neither do I." Linnea paused. She took a few small bites of veggies and a bite of fish. "There are some comfortable rooms in the stables if you'd like to sleep there, or you may sleep in the servants' quarters just down that hall."

"I'll stay in the stables." Kristian loved the smell of horses. He loved horses, period.

"Speak for you yourself." Gracie's eyes shone with delight as she gazed down the hall. "I'll take the servants' quarters."

While Linnea showed Gracie to her room, he meandered down toward the stables. Linnea caught up and led him into a miniature, white bunkhouse beside the stables. The bunkhouse looked like a church building with a bell inside the open-faced steeple.

He couldn't help but notice how clean the bunkhouse was. A calico, patchwork quilt sprawled across a thick double mattress. Pictures of Friesian stallions hung on the dark, rough-hewn walls. One picture was Elliott and Sabrina, and another one was a horse that Kristian figured was Drake, who was as black as night. Besides Drake, there was a mare and a foal with three white stockings.

Linnea lit a small lamp on a table beside the bed.

"You should be quite comfortable here." Her voice was calm and dainty.

"Why did the Dians seem unhappy to see the king?" He stared at her. "I have a weird feeling about him."

"You and everybody else." She cast her eyes down as she fiddled with the quilt. She opened the door, stuck her head out, peeked both ways, and closed it. "We're not sure what to do about it—not yet, anyway." His eyes widened. "I think I can trust you."

Kristian nodded.

She sat down on the edge of the bed. "He's a sly one, that Malakon. One minute he's there, watching you, and the next minute he's gone. You wonder how anybody could disappear that fast, unnoticed. It's eerie. He thinks we don't notice."

"Were you born on Dia?"

Linnea pulled her hair around in front and twisted it until it looked like a corkscrew. "I was born on Lia. Mikal used to be a friend, but he changed since he's been hanging around Malakon. He's not really a bad person. He has anger issues. The death of his parents affected him more than he lets on. He was a loner, I guess you could say, but since Malakon took him in, he acts like a big shot. What about you and Gracie? You two don't exactly seem like two stalks of celery."

He sighed. "We're twins, but we're different as night and day. Seems the only thing we have in common are our parents. Truth is, I don't know what I'd do without her, but I'd never tell her that."

"Tell her."

"Are you kidding? No way."

"The way you feel about her is the way twins are *supposed* to feel; you're supposed to have a close bond. Maybe she feels the same about you, but she's afraid to tell you because she thinks you'll make fun of her. Even so, you shouldn't be so dependent upon her. It's not healthy. You're too old for that. And besides, what would you do if anything ever happened to her?"

Those remarks took him by surprise. He'd never thought of that before. But Linnea just didn't understand what it was like being a twin or having a clubfoot.

Linnea nodded at Kristian's foot as if she had read his thoughts. "What happened?"

"I was born like this." Now he'd get her feeling sorry for him and have her eating out of his hand.

"How do you feel about it?"

"I hate it. Kids tease me."

Her next question surprised him too. "Why do you care about what other people think? And why does your foot bother you so much?"

"What do you mean? Having a foot like this would bother anybody." She didn't understand what it was like. How could she? Just as he was about to change the subject, she reached down and slipped off her tan suede, knee-high boot. Her foot had only two toes: the big toe and the little toe.

His mouth dropped open. He stared. So that's why she limped.

"Why are you staring?"

"Because I… I'm sorry. I don't mean to."

"You see? People stare. It's normal. They're not trying to be mean. It's just a natural response. It doesn't bother me. And it shouldn't bother you either." Her voice was soft and compassionate, but to him, her words sent a different message. "You just need to stop feeling sorry for yourself."

Stop feeling sorry for himself? That was what he did best. But who did she think she was telling him how to feel? "That's kind of rude to say, don't you think? You don't even know me."

"I know well enough that I'm saying it for your own good, just like I'd tell anyone in your position the same thing. You need to discover who you are on the inside and feel good about that. Then, the outward things won't bother you so much. No one can take away anything on the inside of you unless you let them. It's who we are in here that matters." She pointed to her heart. "This is where self-worth comes from, not there." She pointed to his foot. She strolled to the stall door. "Don't sweat the small stuff."

She smiled and closed the door behind her.

"Don't sweat the small stuff." Kristian grunted, but her words lingered. He slid Ruben's silver box from his pocket, slipped the key into the keyhole, took a deep breath, and turned the key.

The lid sprang open. His heart jumped. A small piece of folded paper lay on black velvet. He unfolded it and read the words, "It holds your destiny."

He pulled the piece of paper from his pocket that he had found the day his father disappeared and stuck the two pieces together. "Guard the heart. It holds your destiny."

What could that mean? And how had Ruben gotten the other half of this note? His thoughts swirled as he grasped for any kind of tidbit in order to solve the mystery. He finally drifted off to sleep.

***

The next morning, Kristian wandered up the hill toward the falls. He enjoyed hearing the roar of water. He waded into the swirling water and felt the cool bubbles around his waist. Faded, trumpet-shaped hyssops grew around the pond as if clinging for their lives. Blue and yellow hummingbirds labored to retrieve the last of their juicy nectar. The remains of fading orchids and lilies crackled in the breeze. Even the waterfall didn't seem as strong as when he'd first arrived.

He sat on a rock and gazed at the bright, eastern light in the sky that was still a mystery.

Linnea was also a mystery but intriguing. He preferred her ladylike-ness to Gracie's tomboyish-ness. It was a welcome change. Linnea made sense when she spoke. If people didn't like him because of his foot, why should he care?

He stared at the note. *Guard the heart. It holds your destiny.* He jumped when someone poked his ribs. Sirus chuckled.

"You're funny," he said sarcastically but cracked a smile. "Why didn't you tell me Linnea and Mikal used to be friends? They sure didn't act like it."

"Does it matter?"

"I guess not." He slid the note in front of the donkey's nose. "What do you make of this? How did Ruben get the other half of this note?"

"You don't suppose... You think he's been to—although I can imagine why, but—"

"What?"

"Do you think he's been to Earth?" Sirus gazed into the sky. Soft weeping sounds drifted overhead, followed by a wave of yellow butterflies.

"What's that noise?" Kristian swiveled his head around.

"Sounds like the planet is weeping."

"That's ridiculous. Planets don't weep."

The weeping turned to moans, and Kristian covered his ears. "Now that's scary."

"Sometimes we fail to see things because we allow our minds to be clouded with insignificant distractions. We seek answers in the wrong places. I believe that the butterflies are warning us."

"About what?" He glanced at Sirus, whose eyes bulged, and the base of his ears lay flat like a dog's when it knew it was in trouble. Kristian passed his hand in front of Sirus's blank stare, but he didn't blink.

A shadow swept over them. Kristian felt a chill as he followed Sirus's gaze. The silver box slipped out of his pocket and clanked on the stone path, forcing it open. The two pieces of the note tumbled across the ground. He froze.

NINETEEN

Talons clacked on the path. An eagle spread its wings before tucking them to its white, downy feathers. It landed in unrestrained splendor, drenching the air with a sweet, dewy fragrance. The creature's breast swelled, revealing tender eyes that Kristian hadn't seen on any animal, not even Nick. He remembered seeing the large, white feather drift across the deck of the vessel on their return. It must have been this creature. And Ruben had stowed away.

Ruben sat straight and aloof. He looked like Malakon, but Kristian couldn't be sure who he really was. This man appeared lofty, dressed like royalty. A sleeveless white tunic covered his red, puffy-sleeved shirt. He wore black, knee-high boots over black tights and a black cape draped over his shoulders, with one side tucked behind his sheath.

He dropped the reins, and they landed on the eagle's neck without making a sound. He cupped his hilt with one hand, held his shield in the other, and descended commandingly down the creature's outstretched wing.

Kristian quivered. He had never seen such gallantry, not even in his dad. The man stopped and stared into his eyes. A sudden gust of wind whipped a strand of frothy saliva from the eagle's beak and slapped against Kristian's cheek. He resisted the urge to stroke the creature, talk to it, and befriend it.

The eagle inched its beak toward him in a nonthreatening way as if he could sense Kristian's willingness to befriend it, but Ruben held out his arm and stopped it. Kristian could see his reflection in the creature's black marble eyes.

The man cleared his throat and broke the enchantment between the two. Etched on his rectangular bronze shield was a dove, clutching a clump of wheat in its talons. Engraved beneath the wheat were three tiny golden hearts.

Another shade of darkness shadowed the land.

Kristian froze. Who was this man? Ruben? Malakon? A schemer? Deceiver? Madman? Or was he the true king of Dia? He had a mole beneath his ear just like Kristian.

Sabrina's hooves clicked when she landed. She flared her nostrils. "Leave the boy alone. I will protect him with my life."

Kristian darted his eyes between the two.

Ruben scooped up the two pieces of paper and the silver box and positioned the pieces together. He clenched his jaw. "What do you know about this note?"

"How did you get the other half of that note?" Kristian dug his fingernails into his palms when his lip quivered. He hoped the man wouldn't pull his sword. Maybe he would have if Sabrina hadn't nudged her nose between them.

The eagle flapped its wings and sounded a short, high-pitched scream. It strutted toward Sabrina as if it was about to attack, but she raised her wings over her head and reared. The eagle backed away.

Out of nowhere, a sphere the size of a hot-air balloon floated across the valley, stopping several feet above them. Kristian's mouth dropped open.

"Dad?" He rushed toward the sphere, shouting, jumping up and down, and swinging his hands through the air to reach it. "Dad!"

It was James all right, but when his dad moved his lips, Kristian couldn't hear him speak.

"It's a hologram." Sabrina trod toward him. She turned to Ruben. "What do you know of this? Where's James?"

It appeared that Ruben had slipped into a brief trance. When he finally found his voice, it was stoical. He stared at Kristian.

"*He's* your father? But that's impossible." Ruben glanced at Sabrina. "What's going on? I don't know anything about this. And why did you take her away?"

Kristian glared at him, wondering who the *her* was.

Ruben swirled around. "I told all of you that my brother is not the true king."

"It's not going to work this time, brother." Malakon burst from the castle. Kristian couldn't seem to move as he stared at the king. "You won't get away with it."

Seeing the two of them together now was clear that they were, indeed, twins. The only way to tell them apart was by their clothes.

"He wants you, Kristian." Ruben's nostrils flared as he gripped the boy's wrist. He nodded toward Malakon and then glared at Sabrina. "I'm heir to my father's kingdom, but you wouldn't listen. Look at the monster you've created." He glanced at Kristian. "You and Gracie are in grave danger."

He trounced toward Sabrina, pulling Kristian behind him. He tried jerking his hand away, but the man's grip was too tight.

She flicked her eyes. "My loyalty lies with *her*, not you."

Elliott turned to her. "Where were you the day I left for Earth, when I couldn't find you?"

Dark clouds churned around the edge of the planet. The temperature had dropped, and the wind picked up.

"I—" Sabrina didn't answer him. She flicked her head and stood between Ruben and Malakon.

Malakon raised his voice. "You've always underestimated me, my dear brother, Ruben MacNeal."

Kristian swallowed. "MacNeal?" He took quick, deep breaths as he glared at Ruben. The wind carried the name through the air where it landed stiffly in Kristian's ears. An air bubble stuck in his throat.

"That's right. Now, get out of my way," Malakon said.

"I will not." Sabrina raised her wings high and planted her hooves.

The king shouted at Ruben. "Tell them who you really are, brother."

Ruben sprinted back up on to his eagle and left.

The veiled light caught Kristian's attention. Meme whizzed past Kristian and Sirus, making a boisterous racket. She didn't stop until she landed on one of Sabrina's ear.

Sabrina pricked her ears forward, sending Meme sailing through the air. "I'm so sorry, Meme, you startled me. What is it?"

Meme zipped back and whispered in her ear. Sabrina glanced toward the forest. "Oh, no, but—"

Ruben returned on a majestic, black-as-coal, Friesian stallion, twice the size of Elliott and Sabrina. It glowed faintly like the others. Its thick, midnight mane was long and rippled against its bulging muscles, and its dense fetlocks hid its hooves. The creature was breathtaking.

"Come with me, Kristian. Hurry," Ruben urged.

The pixie flitted over to Kristian. He winced when she pricked his shoulder with her needlelike claws where she sat perched and nodded toward the forest. "Sorry, Sir, but you need to go to the Gate of the Buried Dome with Sabrina, over there."

Sabrina scooped Kristian onto her back. "I'll explain on the way."

"Wait, I want Sirus to come." Kristian looked down.

"Maybe I should just stay—"

Before Sirus finished his sentence, Sabrina plucked him off the ground by his tail and dropped him in front of Kristian. She galloped and jumped off the cliff and flew toward the forest. Kristian scanned the tall redwoods and oaks from one end of the forest to the other. The trees stood menacingly against the dismal, purplish-gray skyscape.

They slowed and stopped just before they entered the forest. A creamy mist snarled across the tangled bramble on the forest floor.

TWENTY

"I need to tell you, I think the shadow is devouring Dia's light, which is draining us of our strength."

Chills crawled across Kristian's skin. "You mean you know about the shadow?"

"I've kept it a secret because I didn't want to frighten anyone, especially the children. I'm not sure, but I think the shadow seeks the golden heart. I think that it knows the heart is the one thing that can destroy it. And I also believe it is after you because you have the heart."

"But how do you know about the heart? Who else knows about it?"

"I'm not sure who else knows." Sabrina ignored his first question and moved her head back and forth before she proceeded into the forest.

Kristian wrapped his arms around Sirus and squeezed. He remembered how crazed the shadow had gotten when he'd held the heart in the air back on Earth.

"I think the shadow is trapped in the forests. If Dia falls to total darkness, it will dissolve the forest boundaries and provide a way of escape to the shadow and its spawns."

"Spawns?" He didn't know about any so-called spawns.

"But they can't go past the edge of the forest either, right?"

"Correct."

Now things made a little more sense. That's why the shadow couldn't escape the forest on Earth.

"I believe the secret to the golden heart lies within the heart itself. And I think the shadow knows it too."

"That heart must hold great power if so many want it," Sirus whispered.

"Maybe the shadow knew my mom had the heart all along, and that's why it roamed *our* forest. Once it knew I had it, it followed me here."

"I think you're right."

Kristian clutched the heart. Dark, gruesome clouds rolled across the sky. "There has to be a way for the shadow to travel between Earth and Dia. But how?"

Sabrina quivered as she glided into the forest, looking cautiously in both directions. The air had turned balmy inside the forest, and the fog had thickened. Kristian could barely see her head.

"Why didn't I just take the heart back to my mom and let her deal with all of this?"

"Because you chose to keep it, and all choices have consequences, good or bad," Sirus said.

Sharp, high-pitched caws penetrated the forest as Sabrina navigated like a stealth bomber, silent and undetected. The caws pierced his eardrum. It sounded like a pterodactyl. He felt the dread of fear twist his stomach into a knot as Sabrina descended through the fog.

She steered precisely around the distorted images of the trees as they glided deeper into the forest.

"Look. That tree looks just like Alon." Black, snarled branches reached up through the fog to the forest canopy. That's when Kristian noticed a giant shadow swooped down from overhead, temporarily blocking what light there was. Kristian ducked. "Whoa, Sabrina, go."

She sped up. The tips of her wings nipped the branches. Sirus's ears flapped against Kristian's arms. The shadow's squawking and hissing intensified. The stink of animal dung stung his nostrils so that he had to bury his face into Sirus's neck.

Sabrina slowed to a halt, flapping her wings as she stayed in one spot. White air poured from her nostrils as she moved her head from one side to the other. Her ribs moved in and out in tempo with her breaths.

"What is—?"

The shadow swooped down and slammed into their side, propelling them through the air. She stumbled and shuffled across the forest floor, throwing Kristian and Sirus, who skidded across pine needles. They pricked Kristian's back. The strong woodsy scent made him sneeze.

Sabrina groaned. Kristian crawled over to her. Blood trickled down the side of her neck. "You're bleeding."

"Pluck some of those red leaves over there and place them on my wound," she whispered. "Hurry."

Kristian gathered the leaves as quick as he could. The shadow swept over them like a 747. He froze as the stench rushed into his lungs. Several yards away, he spotted the lime-colored eye glowing and darting like a search light. He scrambled back to Sabrina and patted the leaves on her wound. "We have to get out of here."

"Let's go." She stumbled to her feet but stayed low to the ground as she weaved around the giant trunks, snapping branches here and there.

Kristian turned. The green eye was racing up behind them. "Faster—it's behind us." He felt her muscles tighten as she raced through the forest. The brownish-green forest floor blurred as they passed. She barely escaped the edge of the forest when the shadow caught up with them.

Kristian shook. He looked back and saw the glowing eye grow smaller as Sabrina raced past the forest edge and sped across a lake. As he caught his breath, he focused on his surroundings, scanning the dreary land that time seemed to have forgotten. Scraggly trees with snarled limbs stretched high into the sky.

The fog had lifted on this side of the forest, leaving them with a fantastical sight: prehistoric creatures everywhere of every species. They appeared nonthreatening, and Sabrina and Sirus didn't seem concerned.

A black castle protruded from the side of a dark, jagged mountainside. Faint glows sprayed from its portals. A waterfall cascaded over the edge of the mountain.

Without warning, Sabrina enclosed him and Sirus with her wings and then dove into a shimmering, light blue circle in the middle of the lake. She moved swiftly through the murky water and within seconds broke the surface of an underground cavern that looked and felt like a tropical paradise. Palm trees protruded from the cave walls, growing upright, and white sand trimmed the lake's edge.

Kristian inhaled the humid, stifling air. Sabrina trod into a large cavern room where a huge, glass sphere took up space in the middle. The sphere revealed the Kingdom of Dia. He slid down her mane and touched the glass with his fingertips as he crept around it.

"I'm sorry to tell you this, but the image of your father in the hologram originated from here. I'm afraid he was only an image. This laser shot a beam that reflected your father's mirage, and it was transported to the sphere from here." She nodded toward the contraption. "My guess is that either Malakon or Ruben, whoever the sinister one really is, watched everything that was going on here on Dia. I can also guess that one of them was trying to discover the whereabouts of the golden heart."

"So this might be the reason why Linnea said that Malakon had acted suspiciously."

Kristian realized that this may have been the reason he'd felt like someone had been watching him. He could see the entire planet from here. Maybe those prying eyes were the king's—and maybe the king knew he had the heart.

"I can't imagine how this place escaped my knowledge," Sirus said.

"Come, it's time we got back to Dia."

Sabrina glided, high above the glassy lake, toward the forest.

Kristian accepted that he might never know what happened to

his father. His heart hurt just thinking about it. He felt like crying, but he didn't dare. Crying wasn't for guys. He rested his head against Sirus. The cool breeze swirled across his face, tickling his cheeks.

How would someone like him ever save a planet? These people had to be crazy to think such a thing.

Something rammed Sabrina. Kristian's head jerked as she floundered. When he turned, he stared terror in its ugly, black eyes. A giant, flying turtle had clamped its teeth onto her wing. She batted her wings, trying to knock the creature off, but its teeth sunk deeper. The creature's black marble eyes pierced Kristian's gaze.

Sabrina grunted and flicked. The beast was relentless. "Use your sword and detach the creature before it shoves us into the forest."

Trembles spiraled across Kristian's skin. His mouth felt chalky. The creature's bloated, yellowish-green underbelly looked like hideous, aged cottage cheese. The turtle jerked, flapped, and growled as it nudged them closer to the forest.

Kristian wrapped Sabrina's mane around his hand and teetered as he stood up. He pulled his sword, closed his eyes, and slashed it through the air. He peeked at the turtle. He'd missed.

"I think it's best to keep your eyes open," Sirus said.

Another swipe and he missed again. This time, he grunted as he lifted the sword. He jabbed it at the creature but barely missed one of the creature's bulging eyes. The turtle continued prodding Sabrina closer to the forest.

"One…two…three." He clutched the sword with both hands this time and swished the sword through the air.

Sirus ducked. "Press the pommel."

Kristian waggled his shaky thumb toward the heart-shaped, crystal emerald bulge in the handle and pinched. A laser shot through the menacing clouds, hitting the creature. Its body twisted and plunged into the murky water with its vindictive eyes fixed on Kristian.

"Thank you," Sabrina said, catching her breath. Reddish-green residue dripped from her bent wing as she flew northward toward the forest. He was so thankful that she had two sets of wings.

He massaged her neck to relax her. "Okay, you can do this. Slow and easy."

"Oh, no, it's the shadow," Sirus warned.

Kristian wrapped his arms around Sirus. A black trail of smog slithered inside the forest wall, screeching like a pterodactyl. Its stench permeated the air as it halted, locking its green eye on them. A stab of pain shot through his clenched his teeth.

The veiled light hovered above the forest, twice the size it had been. He took a deep breath and willed his muscles to relax. The light calmed him. He saw it now as a beacon of hope. The shadow relented and reversed course. It disappeared, leaving a trail of black, stinking soot. Had it sensed the veiled light was near?

TWENTY-ONE

Elliott, Gracie and Linnea were waiting for them on the other side of the forest, high in the air.

Kristian noticed Linnea. She didn't look so ladylike or like a kid now. She wasn't the meek girl who had fixed them dinner in the kitchen last night. She looked heroic as she stood atop Elliott like a warrior, with black tights and a silver breastplate that covered her black, long sleeved top. Her quiver burst with arrows that glowed with bright, purple tips. She looked like a true markswoman and appeared courageous. He envied her bravery.

Sabrina faltered but continued to fly toward the forest. She stopped at the forest wall and looked around. Kristian stroked her quivering neck as she proceeded over the forest. Minutes later, the shadow swished through the forest like the sound of a vacuum. Its green eye sprayed light through the jagged pines. The treetops shimmied as it hurled toward them.

Sirus buried his face in her mane.

"Here it comes. Go!" The pungent odor burned Kristian's eyes. He gripped the base of Sabrina's mane, and pressed her neck. He glanced back as they sped above the treetops. The shadow's skinny, sooty fingers reached after them. Purple streaks swished through the forest, followed by red flames. The arrows pierced the shadow, but they passed through it.

"We're doomed. The arrows aren't working."

Then the shadow screamed so loud that his ears hurt. The black creature rose like a tower, screaming and swirling. The lasting effects of Linnea's purple arrows and red flames gravitated to the creature's middle section. Its scream was blood-chilling before it appeared paralyzed.

Sabrina raced toward Elliott while Linnea shot more arrows. One of the arrows punctured the shadow's green eye. The creature flattened into a black ribbon, growled, and reeled over the treetops as its eye oozed with green liquid until it disappeared in the forest.

Kristian could still smell the stench. "It's coming back."

The shadow dropped in behind them. He looked back and saw its blood-red mouth. Sabrina barely cleared the edge of the forest when the creature nipped at her tail but missed. They caught up to Elliott and raced over the valley where they landed beside the Great Tree.

"That was too close." Sabrina snorted.

Silence drifted over them as they gathered their wits about them. Kristian froze when he noticed every kind of fruit imaginable hanging from the tree. "How could one tree bare different kinds of fruit? And why isn't this tree dying?"

"No one knows," Sabrina said, "but it's the tree we've been eating from."

The more Kristian stared, the more familiar the tree looked. "Lift me up to that high branch, would you?"

Elliott set him on the branch. He plucked an apple and bit into its sweet, juicy ball as he surveyed the sprawling valley.

Brown brick cottages with copper roofs and red brick chimneys were nestled throughout the valley, each on their own small island that seemed to float. Only a wooden bridge covered with vines connected them to land. The yards were well-manicured. The cottages appeared vacant and void of color.

"Where is everybody?" He bobbed his head trying to get a better view.

"Hiding underground," Linnea said. "They all have underground quarters.

"But why are they hiding?"

Elliott lowered him back to the ground. He stared at the jumbled mess of twisted vines and bramble that had wrapped themselves around the trunk like tentacles. He tugged on the vines until he spotted a dark hole big enough for Elliott and Sabrina to fit through. He inched closer. Grey fog swirled across the ground.

Sabrina scraped her hoof. "We need to get out of here. Give me the golden heart."

"What for? No way."

She moved her face in front of his. "There's no time to explain. You must trust me."

"But—"

"What's this about?" Elliott butted in.

"I need to do something I should've done a long time ago. I've wasted enough time. Kristian, please, I'll bring it back safely."

He could smell her hot breath in his face. He stuck his

trembling hand deep into his pocket to retrieve the heart. "Oh, no, it's gone! The heart's gone. I must've dropped it in the lake or something when we were fighting with turtle. Now what?"

"Maybe I can still—Elliott, please take the children back to look for it. I'll be back as soon as I can." Sabrina sprinted, jumped into the air, and disappeared through the ever-shrinking wormhole.

"What is she talking about?" Linnea asked. "What's going on?"

Elliott jumped into the air with the children and headed back toward the forest. A ruckus broke out in the courtyard, and Kristian could hear Ruben and Malakon hollering at each other.

Elliott turned and headed back toward the courtyard. "Stop it, you two. You are family. Now act like it."

"He's no brother of mine," one said. "Stay back or I'll—"

Both men slipped and scraped their blades together. A v-shaped vein protruded from under the skin of Malakon's forehead.

"The Dians trusted you, but you deceived them. You know nothing about being a leader." Ruben shoved Malakon and pointed his sword at him. "You think that heart will give you power to do that?"

The king rustled to his feet. Their blades scraped and screeched, and he pivoted. "You turned her against me."

"She didn't belong to you," Ruben shot back.

Kristian couldn't imagine who they were talking about.

Dark fog snarled its way through the courtyard. Linnea inched down Elliott's tail and dropped to the ground. Kristian followed her.

Malakon escaped Ruben's wrath and dashed inside the castle.

Gracie jumped on Ruben's shoulders. He tried swinging her loose, but she held tight.

"Get off," Kristian shouted. What had possessed her to do that? "You'll get hurt."

She grunted as she clutched Ruben's neck. Her legs swung around. He tripped, and she rolled over him.

"Let go of me," he shouted. "I told you, I'm not the bad guy." He broke her grasp and swung her gently to the ground. Losing his balance, he shuffled backward and fell into a thorny, faded rosebush. "Ouch!"

"Serves you right," Gracie snapped scrambling to her feet as Ruben scuttled off toward the stables. Kristian wondered if she was afraid of anyone.

"You should've helped her," Linnea told him.

"I didn't need it," Gracie shot back.

Kristian stared at their friend. "What are you talking about? I was just about to—"

"Sure." Gracie shook her head.

She turned to Gracie. "And you should let him help."

His sister slapped her hands on her hips and stared at Linnea. "What are you getting at?"

His face grew warm. He felt like clobbering Gracie for acting like that in front of her.

Meme zipped up and interrupted what could've been a bad scene. As she fluttered around Kristian's head, he gently swatted her away like a mosquito. "Meme, stop. I'm not in the mood. We have to find—"

She whispered, "Mikal's in the room below the castle. He has the golden heart."

"What? How'd he—? Come on, Gracie."

His sister took off after him, but Linnea grabbed her wrist. "Let him go."

"Let go of me."

Linnea looked at Kristian. "You need to do this by yourself."

Why was she telling him what to do? Everyone was staring at him. If he refused to go without Gracie, they'd think he was a scaredycat. If he went alone, Mikal would probably do a number on him. He hoped no one could see his hands shaking. "But—"

Gracie glared at her. "Are you crazy? He—"

"Go get the heart." Linnea glanced at Kristian, who finally turned and hobbled to the room below the castle.

He stopped at the door as a rush of nerves curled throughout his body. His heart pounded. He took deep breaths, reached for the door, and nudged it open. Mikal looked to be in some kind of trance, staring at the golden heart that glimmered between his fingertips, and hadn't even noticed him standing there.

Kristian's mouth felt like cotton. He stretched his fingers. Then, as if he couldn't stop himself, he jumped toward Mikal and grabbed his wrist. His legs felt crazy, but he struggled until he managed to rip the heart out of his hand. It pinged against the wall and spun across the floor.

He jumped on Kristian, but Kristian managed to grab his tunic and fling him to the floor. Mikal slid and slammed into the wall. They both leaped for the heart at the same time, but Kristian beat him by mere inches. He scrambled up the steps and tripped. They wrestled until they reached the courtyard, where they both slid to a halt in front of a large crowd. The Dians stood like statues, gazing into the sky. Gracie cupped her hands over her mouth.

Kristian followed their gaze. A bubble of light drifted from the wormhole and descended.

TWENTY-TWO

Sabrina descended like a butterfly, looking like the queen of all lady Friesians and shimmering like a star inside a dazzling aurora. She carried an unknown rider that was a mere shadowy image inside her arched wings.

Kristian dug his nails into his palms. A lilac scent drifted from the bubble. His stomach fluttered. Surely it couldn't be—

Sabrina landed effortlessly and strolled toward him and Gracie. When she unfolded her wings, they gasped. The crowd erupted in oohs and aahs, and then into cheers when they saw her passenger.

"Mom!" Gracie's scream pierced the silence as she ran toward her. Kristian hadn't seen his mom's smile since before his dad had disappeared. It was warm and shone like the sun.

Gwen stared at her children.

Sabrina extended her wing, and Gwen strolled toward them, her tan cloak rippling across the ground. Her long, auburn hair hung in waves around her shoulders. Gracie rushed into her mother's slender arms.

Gwen hugged her while she gave Kristian a tender glance. He wanted to feel the warmth of her arms too, but she had kept too many secrets from them. She had mentally abandoned them after their father disappeared.

"My lady," the Dians shouted and bowed. "You've returned."

My lady? Kristian swallowed the soft lump in his throat. Gwen scanned the crowd with her warm smile. Her bottom lip quivered, and her eyes glistened.

"You've known about this place all along." His cheeks grew hot, and he clenched his jaw.

"Please, let me explain," Gwen said.

"He'll get over it, Mom." Gracie glared at him. "Won't you?"

"It hasn't been the same without you." Elliott nuzzled Gwen's arm. "I was on my way to Earth when I saw Kristian in trouble. I rescued him, but I didn't know what to do, so I brought him here."

"Thank you. You did the right thing." She closed her eyes and inhaled as she swirled in a circle. But when she stopped, her face froze. "Where's James?"

"I'm sorry, my lady, but he hasn't returned."

Gwen shook her head. "No, that can't be. I thought for sure he had returned."

"Mom, what's going on?" Kristian glared at her.

"Yeah, I'm with him." Gracie stared at her. "What's going on?"

Before Gwen had a chance to respond, Sabrina interrupted them. "Dia's been growing darker since your father's disappearance."

Kristian tightened every muscle in his body.

"What happened?" Gwen pressed her hand to her cheek and walked over to Sabrina. They mumbled between themselves.

Gracie stomped toward them. "You mean our grandfather lives

here?"

Their mother nodded. "Yes, King Aaron."

"I thought Dia would get its light back when you returned." Sabrina hung her head. "But it didn't work."

"But my father told me I couldn't return without the golden heart," Gwen murmured. "How did you know I could?"

"I didn't for sure, but I had a strange feeling. It was worth a try. I only wish I had thought of it earlier."

Gwen turned toward the stables. She brought her hand to mouth and whimpered. "Sabrina, take me to him."

Sabrina flew Gwen to the stables. Kristian watched from a distance, as she slid down, slipped her cape off, and tossed it to the ground. She strolled toward Ruben with her arms extended. He placed a sword across her outstretched hands. She grasped the handle, stepped back, and quick as lightning, brandished the sword like a skilled swordswoman—thrusting it this way and that, outward, behind her, up and over her head. She did it so fast it made Kristian's head spin.

Kristian caught Linnea smiling at his mother as if reminiscing about earlier times.

Gwen pivoted. She ended her routine with a delicate arm curved over her head while she pointed the sword in the air with the other. She bowed her head and stepped back before handing the sword back to Ruben, gripping Sabrina's mane, and mounting her with the greatest of ease.

Kristian felt Sirus's warm body against his leg.

Sabrina returned, and Gwen slid off. He eyed his mother as she strolled over to Linnea and gave her a hug. She turned and walked to him.

"I know you're upset, and you've every right to be. But time is running out." Her voice sounded feeble. "After speaking with Ruben, things are worse than I expected." She unfolded her fingers like a flower petal on a warm spring day. He gave me this." She held a small, rectangular, copper box. "Sabrina and Ruben believe you've been chosen to save Dia from the shadow. And my heart agrees."

His mom's smile made him believe he could conquer the world, but he felt that she had a heavy heart behind that smile. "But why me?"

Gwen placed the copper box in his palm. "Open it. Slowly."

As Kristian inched open the lid, fluorescent colors streaked through the crack upward through the sky. At the end of the light, was a sign of a cross with the word *Ithfa* written across the arms. He gasped.

"Faith," he whispered.

Sirus cleared his throat. "Don't—"

"Shhhh." Kristian closed the lid.

Sirus waddled off with his head hanging.

Gwen gazed into his eyes. "My destiny was to be the queen of Dia if anything happened to father. He handed me the golden heart for my specific destiny. He knew that something was destroying the planet. I was to discover what it was and try to stop it. When the golden heart went missing, I panicked. I thought I'd be stranded on Earth forever. Now, the golden heart is gone, along with James."

He stared at her and swallowed hard. "But I don't want your

destiny. I want to know what happened to Dad."

She shook her head. "I don't know, and that's the truth."

Kristian darted his eyes between Sabrina and Elliott. They had been looking suspicious. "What do you two know of this?"

They remained silent.

"How do you know about this place, Mom?" He shoved the box back in her hand. "You know what? Just forget it. I don't want to know. I've had enough of all this secretive nonsense. I just want to go home."

"Yeah, me too." Gracie stomped her foot.

Sabrina stepped forward and whispered in his ear. "Did you find the heart?"

"Yes, Mikal had it."

"Show your mother."

He gasped. He felt his face grow hot. "Why did you have to say that?"

"Show me what?" Gwen asked.

"She has a right to know."

"Just like we had a right to know about all of this?" He swung his hand through the air. His stomach twitched. He took a deep breath and slipped the golden heart from his pocket. Gracie's eyes were the size of walnuts. He stretched out his arm and uncurled his fingers.

Gwen flung a hand over her mouth. "*You* had it?"

Kristian drew his eyes to the heart. Now she knew the ugly truth. "After I went to the forest, I found it, but I got swept away by Elliott."

His face grew hotter. He hobbled down a worn path and didn't stop until he reached the pines.

Gwen caught up to him, clasped his arm, and twirled him around. "I'm so relieved the heart is safe." She hugged him. Her warm arms felt safe. "I've been frantic these past months, thinking it could be in the wrong hands. And I'm so thankful you two are safe. My father believed the heart held power. I believe the power of the heart will save Dia."

"How do you know that?"

"I discovered it in one of Dia's history books one day in an ancient library I found here. I believe what my father said, that the heart holds a secret. And we must find the key that opens it." Her voice quivered.

"A library?" Kristian's breath quivered in his throat. Libraries held all kinds of secrets, at least to those who weren't knowledgeable about history. He was intrigued with them, especially old ones. He even liked the smell. And the thought of an ancient one thrilled him.

"I was skeptical, but now I believe you really were born for this moment in time. One of the books speaks about a grandson to King Aaron, my father. And you've inherited my destiny. Now you will fulfill it."

Pinpricks tingled across his arms and neck.

"I believe the secret has to do with you, Kristian, though I'm not sure what." Wisps of her hair blew in the gentle breeze. Her eyes looked glazed, as if she had drifted to another place in time.

Determined, Kristian was going to find the underlying cause of her melancholy absences. "None of it makes any sense."

Gwen wrung her hands and paced while the others remained silent. "Just because things don't make sense doesn't mean they're meaningless. When things don't make sense, that's when we need the faith to know that there's more to it than we can see."

Kristian remained silent.

"Faith sprouts from within us, and we must still choose to believe even when something doesn't make sense. And   "

"And the path that lies behind us is usually darker than the hope-filled path that lies ahead." Kristian had no idea where those words just came from. He stared at his mom's flawless, golden beauty. "I just need to think."

He hobbled down the path in search of Sirus. His friend's long, S-shaped tail twitched across the path. The little donkey was securely snuggled beneath a blueberry bush, but this time, there weren't any chomping sounds. He grabbed Sirus's tail and slid him out from beneath the bush. His hooves covered his face.

"I'm sorry for shushing you back there." Kristian's heart sank. "Come on. You don't need to hide."

He stooped down and tugged Sirus's hooves off his face. That's when he discovered the real reason Sirus was hiding his face. His mouth looked like one giant grape.

"Not again." Kristian sighed. "Okay, come on. I think something big is about to happen, and I want you with me when it does." Sirus rolled over and began kicking. Kristian formed his hands into bear claws and scratched.

Sirus smiled and wrestled to his feet. His eyes gleamed like waxed, black cherries. Thunder rumbled, and Kristian glanced up and noticed the warbling wormhole had grown smaller.

Gwen twisted her hands as Kristian and Sirus approached. "I'm sorry for putting you and Gracie— Well, let me just say, plain and simple, my time on Earth was up."

"What do you mean your time was up?" The twins asked in unison.

"I—"

The castle doors burst open. Meme and the Pippins carried Malakon haphazardly out of the castle toward the forest.

"You won't get away with this," Malakon said, shaking his fist and kicking.

"We shall lock him in his own castle so he won't be causing any trouble," Meme said.

"And stay there," Ruben shouted as his eagle's talons clicked on the courtyard. Gwen wrenched her dress in her hands. He dismounted and rushed to her. "Are you okay?"

She nodded.

"Why did you leave Dia?" he asked her.

"There's no time to explain. We have to find the key to the heart before it's too late."

Hooves pounded the cobblestone path. Mikal pulled on the reins of his steel gray, white-socked steed and rushed to Gwen. Ruben stepped in front of him, and Mikal jerked to a halt.

"Go on. Tell them why you left," Mikal urged her.

Ruben cupped the top of his hilt. "Leave her alone."

Gwen fidgeted and fumbled with the button on her dress. Mikal's royal blue eyes turned midnight blue. He pulled his sword. Kristian gripped his own.

"Put the sword away," Ruben said.

"I loved you." Mikal stared at her. "I waited twelve years for you to return, and even now, after all this time, you still have eyes for *him*." He fumbled with the key that dangled from the end of a rope tied around his waist as he nodded toward Ruben.

She swallowed and stepped from behind Ruben then took a deep breath and placed her hands on her hips. "I don't have to explain anything to you, do you understand? For you to think that I had eyes for you is crazy. I suggest you get back on your steed and don't ever bully me again."

Mikal pointed his sword at Ruben, who clenched his jaw. "Tell them the truth, Gwen."

Her mouth twitched, and her shoulders shook. She didn't look so princess-like now.

TWENTY-THREE

Gwen ambled toward her children as if she were dizzy. "Before I went to Earth—"

"Before you went to Earth?" Kristian and Gracie both interrupted.

Her fingers fumbled along the bodice of her dress. She glanced at Ruben. "I…we…we're—"

"What?" Kristian asked.

"We're…Dian. This is my home—your home. Our heritage. I wanted to visit Earth before you were born, but my father was against it. After he realized how desperate I was to go, he allowed it, but only if James accompanied me." She stepped closer to them. "My father gave me the golden heart and told me it was the only way I could return to Dia. He warned me to keep it safe. So I gave it to James for safekeeping. But when he disappeared, I thought the heart was lost for good and I'd never be able to return to Dia. I was so terrified and felt so alone. My thoughts consumed me like a fire, day and night."

Guilt rushed over Kristian like a waterfall. "You mean that's why you starred at the forest all that time? That's why you ignored us?"

She nodded then whimpered. "I didn't mean to ignore you. I can't change the past. I've lost precious time with you both—time spent wondering if I'd ever find the heart or James again."

Kristian swallowed hard.

"Why didn't you just tell us?" Gracie blurted.

He wiped his top lip. "I didn't think we were important to you."

The corner of Gwen's mouth quivered. "Oh, heavens, no. I never meant that. When I left Dia, we—"

She reached for their hands, glanced at Ruben again, and then held out her hand. He clasped her hand in his. She gazed into her children's eyes.

"Ruben is—" Her voice crackled. She glanced at Ruben. "Ruben is your real father."

Silence strangled Kristian. He stared at Gracie's chalky-colored face. So that's why he, Ruben, and Malakon had moles below their ears, why they had the same last name. He didn't want to believe it.

"My father never trusted Ruben, so I knew he wouldn't approve of our marriage. That's—"

"Then who's James?" Gracie asked. Kristian gritted his teeth.

"Your uncle...my brother. But James never wanted to be involved in any of this. He did it for me."

"No." Gracie stomped her foot. "James is our dad. How could you keep that from us?"

Kristian felt no heartbeat. It was as if someone had ripped it out. That's why he'd never seen his mom and James kissing. He looked at Ruben. Things were making more sense. "How can we ever trust you again, Mom?"

"This is crazy." Gracie rubbed her eyes. "Somebody tell me

this is a nightmare."

Kristian glared at Ruben, whose face had turned ashen.

Gwen turned to him too. "I'm sorry I had to leave. I couldn't endure your anger with your brother or my father controlling my life. I couldn't have our children grow up around such a poisonous atmosphere."

Ruben put his hands on his hips, turned his back to her, and hung his head. Evidently, he hadn't known.

Mikal lurched at Gwen. She whirled around and shoved her palm in his face. "Stop!"

He jerked to a halt and stumbled backward.

She stomped toward him and waved her hand in front of his face. "You have bullied me enough. Leave me—us—alone."

Ruben jerked Mikal's arms behind his back and scurried him back to the castle. Kristian stomped off.

"James is our dad." Gracie bolted past Kristian, flinging her arms in the air. "You're all liars, all of you."

She despised lies. And now, he did too. Lies could destroy people and hurt people. His mom's lies had cut his heart in half.

"Wait." He felt the breeze as Gwen rushed past him to catch Gracie. She threw her arms around her daughter and rolled across the ground. Gracie thrashed her legs and arms.

"Let me go." She grunted.

Kristian pulled the golden heart from his pocket and shoved it at his mom, who held Gracie tight and heaved. "Whose heart is this?"

"I told you. It's your grandfather's." She swallowed and

smacked her lips as she tried to catch her breath.

Elliott and Sabrina trotted up. "Go on, tell them, Sabrina." Elliott said.

Gwen jumped up and rushed to Sabrina. "What is it?"

"My lady, your father... Well, he had found the golden heart beside the Great Tree in the valley one day."

"Go on." Gwen furrowed her brows.

"He didn't know I was hiding near the tree, watching. When he picked the heart up, it glowed and then faded. I overheard him tell Mikal that he thought the heart had some kind of power. I thought it was only the thoughts of an...sorry, an old man. Excuse me, my lady." Gwen waved the remark away. "I never gave it a second thought until now."

Kristian stared at his foot. He clenched his teeth so hard the pain shot through his gums to his roots. He jammed his fingernails into his palms and glared at Sabrina. "You mean an old man thought this heart had power just because it glowed? Are you kidding me?" He kicked a stone. He had been clinging to a hope that the heart could fix his foot. "The heart's a fake."

Gwen cupped her mouth and gasped. "Oh, what have I done?"

Ruben placed his hand on her shoulder. "You've done nothing wrong. I'm the one who failed all of you—all of Dia."

He glanced at the children. Sirus waddled over to Gracie and wiggled his butt in the grass beside her. He sat silently and allowed her to use him as a pillow for her tears. She wasted no time burrowing her face into his mane.

"James is our dad," she garbled into his neck.

Kristian sat next to his sister. In a halfhearted attempt, he slipped his arm around her shoulder. She was a tomboy, but on the inside, she was a daddy's girl. Right now, she was his twin, and his heart wept with her heart. He could feel her pain.

"James will always be our dad. No one can change that." He peered at Ruben. Something had happened to James. Kristian believed he was still alive, somewhere... he hoped.

Elliott lumbered up to Sabrina. "You took them to Earth? Is that why I couldn't find you that day? Do you know how worried I was?"

"I'm sorry," she said. "But I gave Gwen my word I wouldn't say anything to anyone, not even you."

He drooped his head and clopped off. She sighed. The wind curled the thick clouds through the blueberry and raspberry sky. The wormhole continued to shrink.

Gwen drew Kristian away from the others. "I know I've hurt you. And I'm so sorry. I was wrong for not telling you and Gracie the truth. I believe Dia is dying because of me."

"Why because of you?"

"Ruben wasn't the only reason I left Dia. My father was so overprotective and controlling of all of us. We became so dependent on him that it almost ruined me. His intentions were good, but—" Her sea green eyes glistened. "Didn't you notice how stoic the Dians are? It's as if their minds are numb to emotions. I believe the heart is the only power that will save this planet and its people."

Her voice faded as he watched the veiled light drift in and out of the dense clouds. His surroundings became obscure as he focused on its light, pink glow. It seemed like a silent voice was speaking to his heart again as he stared at the light: *Be not discouraged, have faith.*

Gwen's voice came back to life. ". . . and furthermore—I believe you've been chosen to unlock the secret of the golden heart."

Ghoulish screams pierced the dusky sky. They came from the forest. Orange eyes broke through the dark clouds. A vulture carrying Malakon flew overhead. "Did you think anyone could lock me in my own castle?"

Sabrina shrieked. "The Pippins. Where are they?"

TWENTY-FOUR

The Friesians flared their wings and reared. Kristian felt the vibration when their hooves hit the ground. Gwen stood with her back against Kristian and wrapped her arms around his waist.

"Leave him alone. Take me instead."

"Oh, my lady, you are of no importance to me now." Malakon's laughter resounded.

She turned and prodded Kristian's shoulders. "Run. Don't stop!"

He hobbled so fast that his body got ahead of his legs, and he tumbled headlong. Ruben scooped him up before he hit the ground. Kristian's toes scraped across the grass as Ruben sprinted toward the falls.

"Malakon wants the golden heart," Ruben murmured. "He wants its power."

"Let me go. I don't need your help. And it doesn't have any power!"

Ruben slid to a halt at the edge of the cliff. "Yes, it does. Keep it safe." Mist swirled around them, and Kristian looked down at the frothy, thunderous water. The black vulture circled.

"You're not getting him," Ruben shouted. Kristian heaved and tried to squirm loose.

"Give me the heart, and no one will get hurt," Malakon ordered.

"Grab my waist and don't let go," Ruben whispered.

Kristian stared down at the lake and then shut his eyes. "No, I can't do it."

The man gripped Kristian's waist and leaped into the mist. Kristian's stomach rushed up to his chest. The vulture dove through the mist, and Kristian lost sight of it until it flew out of the mist and plucked him from Ruben's grasp.

He flailed, upside down in the creature's beak. Blood rushed to his head, and he lost sight of Ruben in the vaporous cloud.

The vulture soared over the forest and glided across the lake. It dove into the murky water below the dark mountain that he had seen earlier in the side of the cliff. The warm, bitter liquid stung his throat. Just when he thought he'd lose consciousness, they surfaced in an underground cavern.

The vulture dropped him onto the bumpy bedrock. He shivered as he rolled across the damp ground. Water trickled over the walls, shimmering from a lit torch nearby. He stared at the stagnant water, some bones, fragments of a shabby knight's armor, a shield, and a rusty breastplate—the remains of a knight, no doubt.

A cold breeze pushed past them. He trembled as he peered down a dark tunnel.

Malakon tossed a tattered, gray blanket to him and glowered. "I'm not going to hurt you, lad." He sat down on a large rock. "I brought you here for your safety. You must trust me. They're not your friends." He nodded towards Dia. "They only want the heart."

He gripped the blanket tighter. "They *are* my friends."

The king shook his head. He answered, "No," before lumbering toward Kristian. He halted. "Ruben knows the throne belongs to me. He's fooled your mother into thinking he's the good guy. Give me the heart, and I'll keep it safe for you. You must trust me."

Should he trust him? His queasy gut said no. He flicked his eyes toward the menacing tunnel. It looked like his only way out.

"Give me the heart." Malakon held out his hand. "You want to save Dia, don't you?"

Kristian wet his lips. Sirus's words drifted through his mind— *it is better to flee your enemies than be overcome by them.* The veiled light moved slightly inside the tunnel. He tugged up his pants. Just as he was about to run, the man's eyes glistened.

"You know," the man said in a calm voice, "the golden heart can save this kingdom, lad, and the power the heart holds will only work in the hands of a true king. That's why you must give it to me." He stretched his arm out. "Give me the heart, and you'll see that I am the true king of Dia."

Kristian clutched the heart. The man was lying. His eyes gave him away. His mouth twisted, and his laugh turned eerie. His face grew solemn as he stared at Kristian and slipped off his boot to reveal a clubfoot.

"Yes, *I* am your father." He replaced the boot, and Kristian felt like he was going to vomit. Malakon's eyes became expressionless as if his mind had drifted to another time. "I had to fight for my father's affections. He loved my brother more and treated him better than me. I waited so long for my father to tell me he loved me, but he never did." He felt the man's pain. "Now, give me the heart, so I can make my father proud of me."

Kristian felt sorry for him. He slipped the heart from his pocket and touched the king's shoulder, but Malakon whacked his hand and sharpened his gaze. With one eye closed, he said, "Don't touch me."

The man seized his wrist, and Kristian trembled. He clutched the heart. Flashes of blinding yellowish-red light sprayed through the slits of his fingers as he tried to pry his fingers apart. The golden heart was ablaze, but it wasn't burning Kristian's hand. Malakon pried open the last finger and grabbed the heart. He screamed and hurled the heart, which clinked across the wet stone. The man clutched his hand to his chest.

"Why did it burn me?" White froth pooled in the corners of his mouth. His face turned red as if someone was strangling him. He clutched his neck. Kristian scooped up the heart and raced down the tunnel after the veiled light.

"Stop," Malakon screamed. "We must stay calm. Maybe that's how the heart reacts when it's in the hands of a true king." Footsteps clomped down the tunnel. "Come back. Drop the heart into my pocket."

Moist air clung to Kristian's face as he reached the end of the tunnel behind a waterfall. He rubbed his aching foot as he caught his breath. Behind him, talons clicked, and a bird screamed as the sound of wings brushed against the walls.

He turned and could see the eagle's white fleece through the darkness. The eagle and the vulture clashed. Someone yanked on his shirt and tugged him farther behind the falls.

"You still have the heart?" Linnea asked.

He sighed. "Yes. What are you doing here?"

"Faith without works is dead." She carried her bow and a quiver filled with arrows.

"What do you mean?"

The vulture and an eagle flailed down the tunnel, squawking. Their talons clicked across the rocky terrain, and a few feathers flew through the air as Ruben and Malakon tried to control their creatures. The eagle tore into the vulture's flesh with its talons, and the vulture screamed.

"What happened?" Linnea asked.

He told her everything. "How do we know who's the real king?"

"Right now, we don't."

Kristian rushed from behind the falls. Linnea tried grabbing his arm but missed. "Wait."

"One of you loved my mom." He stepped in front of the two men. The creatures bumbled to a stop and stared at him in silence. "Why didn't one of you stop her from leaving this place?"

Moments of silence felt like minutes. Then Ruben blurted out, "I didn't know she left. I searched for hours looking for her, but I couldn't find her."

"You're lying," Malakon shouted.

Ruben struggled to keep the eagle quiet. He glanced at Kristian. "Real love makes no demands on anyone. I didn't try to stop her because no one can force anyone to love them."

Restless, both creatures clapped their talons on the rocky shoreline, batting their wings as they faced each other. Malakon jumped off his creature and raced toward Kristian.

As he tried wrestling the heart from him again, sparks from the heart seared stripes across the man's face. Kristian suspected that the heart was responding to someone who was not the king of Dia. The man's face turned into the most horrible of horribles, with bulging eyes and red, plump cheeks. It was like looking into a Christmas bulb.

Malakon stumbled into the water. A wave crashed over him and he never resurfaced.

"Come on," Ruben shouted. "We've wasted enough time. You'll have to trust me."

Kristian looked at Linnea.

"We don't have a choice," she said. "Together we'll trust him."

"But what if—"

"Then together we'll fight him. Deal?"

He nodded. "What about the heart?"

She dove into the water. After several minutes, she popped back up and handed the heart to him. "Here. Keep it safe."

"Thanks." He shoved the heart into his pocket, and they scrambled up on the eagle. Halfway over the lake, Malakon waited for them in the sky. He was on another creature that resembled SanDorak, only it was white.

Kristian tightened his arms around Ruben's waist. Ruben yanked on the reins, and the eagle halted.

"Help!" a voice squealed across the stillness.

"He's got Gracie!" Sweat beaded on Kristian's forehead.

The eagle's short, high-pitched whistles pierced the sky. The eagle was so courageous. The white dinosaur shot thick, fiery streams through the air.

"Give me the heart, and she won't get hurt."

Gracie jerked her arm from the man's grasp and plunged into the lake, screaming all the way down.

"Go and save your sister," Ruben said. "I have to attend to my brother."

"But I can't swim."

"Come on. We can do this. Don't be afraid." Linnea took Kristian's hand and jumped.

"But—" He flailed and screamed until they hit the water then thrashed his arms and legs as he fought to surface. Linnea gripped his shirt and dragged him to the top. He gasped.

"You okay?" She heaved.

He shook his head, kicked, splashed, and then sputtered. In the process, he accidentally shoved her under. She popped back up.

"Stop fighting it. Calm down, and we just might succeed. Take a deep breath. Let the water embrace you. Tread lightly."

He nodded and did as she said. The blurry image of the veiled light near the shore calmed him.

"Take a breath. Stay with me. And most important, stay calm."

He nodded as he took a deep breath and slipped beneath the water beside Linnea. So far, so good. She tugged on his arm and pointed to some weeds tangled around Gracie. They swam down to her.

TWENTY-FIVE

Someone's hands thrusted his back, and water spewed from his mouth. He coughed, spit, sputtered, and gagged. When he rolled over, he saw Gracie's wet face through a foggy haze. "You're safe."

"Yes, no thanks to you." She shook her head. "I had to help Linnea drag you to the surface after she untangled me."

The eagle's screams ripped through the sky. They glanced up as it gripped the side of the dinosaur's neck and swung it full circle. The eagle released the white beast and hurled it through the air. The dinosaur scowled. Blood splattered on top of the lake. All the prehistoric creatures that had gathered on the shore stood silent and unmoving.

The dinosaur batted the eagle with her tail, sending it—and Ruben—through the sky. The eagle returned and clasped its talons into the dinosaur's flesh and spun it until it had become a white blur then let go. It rolled, flipped, toppled, and mowed a giant swath of pines through the forest that fell like dominos. Waves crashed against the shoreline. The eagle swooped down, but just as it was about to pluck the trio from the shoreline, it retreated.

"Look out behind you," Ruben shouted.

Kristian could already smell the rotting stink. "It's okay. The creature can't penetrate the forest's edge."

Ruben swooped, picked them up, and soon landed in the courtyard.

Gwen hurled her arms around her children. "Thank goodness you're safe."

Warriors on black stallions were assembling in the sky around Dia's perimeter. White stallions surrounded the south perimeter. Something told him he would soon discover Dia's fate. His legs grew feeble.

***

Kristian hobbled to the white book in the foyer. He shuffled through the pages and narrowed his eyes. There had to be a clue. He flipped, blinked, and flipped again. Then he stopped.

It was as if an invisible finger was writing on the page. Shiny, gold letters appeared in some sort of ancient, beveled words. "Hope, the substance of things hoped for, the evidence of things not seen, saved in a heart that listens and believes and a beacon for the hopeless."

His throat tightened. He looked around but didn't see anyone. Although it felt like someone was watching him. He turned the page. More words appeared. "What and who you believe in will decide your life's path…"

The words faded. He flipped the page. A sandstone castle appeared with two golden, heart-shaped doors. One of the doors stood ajar. He flinched when something bumped against his leg.

Sirus sighed. "It's about time. What do you see?"

"A mustard tree growing near the entrance of a castle."

"What else?"

Kristian leaned closer. "A tiny, silver skeleton key. And it's pulsating."

"Your destiny begins not a moment too soon, I dare say." The little donkey waddled across the floor and stopped in the doorway.

"What do you mean?" Kristian turned and noticed another white pedestal on the other side of the foyer, but there was no book on top.

"We've little time," Sirus said. "Come along."

"Where are we going?"

"You've just discovered where the key is. You must retrieve it."

"But I don't know where that castle is."

"If I told you then it would be my journey and not yours. Dia's fate lies in your hands."

Kristian hobbled back to the book and studied the picture. A lilac scent drifted through the doorway. His mom's tan cape glided across the floor, and the warm glow in her eyes from a candle comforted him. A slight quiver ran down his back. There was nothing like a mother's love.

Gracie, Sabrina, and Elliott squeezed through the door at the same time and got stuck. His sister pushed, grunted, and squeezed through them until they all stumbled in and fell in the foyer.

Sirus shook his body. "Dia's light is fading. And since you and Gracie are considered half-Dian and half-Earthling, I'm afraid you, too, will begin to lose your strength."

"But how can that be if Ruben is our father, and he's Lian?"

The donkey waddled back beneath the Friesians' legs. He was already down the steps when he called over his shoulders. "Because you both were raised on Earth, you've taken on many Earthly traits. Now, we must get to the forest, quick."

"Out of my way." Elliott pushed past Sabrina as he clopped out the door.

"Wait for me." Gracie dashed out behind them.

They all flew to the forest wall. Kristian glimpsed the veiled light through the trees and nudged Sirus.

"I see it," Sirus said.

It had grown bigger since Kristian had last seen it.

"There are two trees in this forest, and they're different than all the rest," Sirus said. "One's in the north; one's in the south. And all I know is that one of them is a door to finding what you seek."

"Great." Kristian peered into the gloomy shadows. Goosebumps pricked his neck. "But how do I know which tree to choose? Can't you just tell me which one it is, and save me some time and trouble? Why does everything have to be such a big mystery?"

"You must learn to train your senses. It's all part of the journey, and mainly because I don't know either."

He shook his head, stretched his shirt away from his neck, and took a deep breath.

Sabrina squeaked her hoof across the moist grass. "Can you get them to the tree, Elliott?"

"Yes, but it'll have to be swift." He glanced both ways. A guttural growl sounded in the distance like it was from the pit of the earth.

Kristian wiped his forehead as his frustrations mingled with his fears. Dia's light was dwindling, and the air was thick. A milky mist rolled across the forest floor. Without warning, the sky released a downpour of warm rain, drenching them. Within minutes, Sirus's mane looked like a long, flat ribbon. Kristian squinted and stared into the gray forest.

"Listen to the still, small voice," Sirus reminded him.

"Come with me," he told Sirus.

"I'm sorry, but I cannot accompany you this time."

"Sabrina? Ruben?"

"Sorry," Sabrina said.

"I'll come," Gracie said.

"No." He pretended he didn't want her to come, but he hoped she would.

"Doesn't matter what you say; I'm coming anyway."

Thank you, he thought but sneered. "You'd just better stay out of my way then."

Gracie grinned. Kristian glanced at his mom, her wet hood clinging to her head. She smiled. He wanted to tell her he loved her, but a clap of thunder distracted him.

"Ready?" Elliott reared.

Kristian shoved his wet hair back off his forehead. "I guess."

"Which way?"

"I say we go that way, east." Gracie blurted, nodding.

"It doesn't matter what you say. This is *my* destiny." The veiled light floated, as if it were prodding them to go in the direction that Gracie wanted to go, but how could he go that way now after she suggested it? He couldn't. A sharp twinge pricked his neck. "I say we go that way, west."

Wet leaves slapped against their faces as Elliott raced toward the west. Kristian glanced back. The veiled light had eluded them.

Elliott halted in front of the giant tree as he slid across the wet ground. "Okay, down you go. Hurry. I must get out of here before—"

A creature screamed. The children slipped down. The tree's leaves rustled in the cool breeze and dark swirls along the tree's trunk looked like gruesome faces. Kristian glanced around but didn't see the veiled light.

"Come on," Gracie said.

"Wait." He grabbed her wrist when he spotted the glare of the green eye through the trees on the other side of the forest. "Elliott, take us to the east tree."

"I told you this wasn't the right way," Gracie grumbled. They turned, but Elliott was gone. "Now what?"

Kristian looked around and thought he saw a green glow. "It's coming! Run—this way." He slapped branches out of his way as they ran down the path toward the edge of the forest.

"It's right behind us." Gracie tripped and fell. "You should've listened to me."

The eye was nearly upon them. He gripped the back of her shirt and dragged her across the bramble until she found her footing. Just as the creature opened its red mouth, they tumbled out of the forest.

The shadow flattened as if it rammed into a wall. It growled. Kristian could feel the creature's wretched breath. "Elliott!"

The Friesian swooped down. "What happened?"

"It wasn't the right tree."

"Okay. Let's go."

"Thank you," Gracie snapped.

They slid to a halt in front of the tree in the east. Kristian spotted the green eye scurrying toward them. They dropped on the ground and stood in front of the gnarled tree. He looked through the dense leaves. The veiled light waved near a tall branch.

"Okay, let's go in," he mumbled. "Elliott—" Kristian turned. Elliott was gone. "Again?"

The shadow roared, and branches snapped.

He tugged vines away from the opening, and Gracie pitched in. They stumbled inside. The trunk was dark as night. She slipped her hand into his back pant pocket, and he didn't resist. They patted the inside of the tree's cold and slimy trunk.

The creature's shriek pierced the silence, and the tree glowed green outside the entrance.

"Nothing's happening," she said.

"It has to be the right tree." He slapped the tree as he turned in a circle. The shadow screeched again. He pounded the tree. "Nothing's happening."

The shadow screamed and almost blew Kristian's eardrums out of his head. His hands trembled along the cold wood. The ground shook, and the tree vibrated. The leaves wrestled as if a violent storm was coming. He unconsciously clutched Gracie's arm, his other hand skimmed across a large knot in the tree, and seconds later, the ground dropped out from beneath them.

They gripped each other's hands as they flailed down into the depths of the cold tree trunk. Kristian's stomach rushed into his throat. A deafening silence swallowed them before streaks of white light whizzed past them.

Several seconds later, they plunged into water, and it rushed up Kristian's nose. He gagged, spit, and thrashed. The tips of his toes barely touched the mucky bottom. He flapped his arms to stay above the surface. He gagged on a slimy piece of seaweed. At a slapping sound, he asked, "Gracie, is that you?"

"No, I'm on shore already. Hurry up."

"I'm drowning!" He flailed his arms through the water.

"I'm coming."

The noise grew louder as water gurgled down his throat. Gracie grabbed his shirt and tugged him toward shore.

"Calm down. Kick your feet or you'll drown us both."

When they finally reached shore, the noise stopped. Kristian lay back and gasped as snot ran down the back of his throat. The only sound he heard now was the sparse croak of frogs and chirping crickets.

Gracie shoved her hair off her face. "Where are we?"

He sat up and glanced around. "I don't know, but the key has to be here somewhere. Let's find that castle, grab the key, and get out of here. Look, over there—it's dad's rowboat."

"We're back home again." Gracie took off, and he hobbled

behind her. But something felt funny. It was as if they were running in slow motion.

"We're losing strength," he said.

They struggled onto the front porch of their house, bent over and clutching their stomachs until they caught their breath. They stumbled through the front door.

"Mom!" Gracie yelled.

"She's not here. She's back on Dia."

"Then what are those voices upstairs?"

They crept up the stairs and stopped outside his bedroom. Their mouths dropped open, and their eyes widened as they stared at the scene before them. The dim glow from the table lamp sprayed through the bedroom and into the hall. The only thing that separated them from the past was a thin film as the scene unfolded: it was the morning before Kristian had run off. His bedroom door had slammed against the wall and bounced back against Gracie's palm.

The children watched the past as Gracie folded her arms and tapped her foot. "You're such a nerd."

"Get out of my room." Past-Kristian shouted at her.

She tromped across his scattered clothes and glared out his window toward the forest. "Mom told you to stay away from there. One of these days you'll be sorry when the same thing that happened to Dad happens to you—you'll just *poof!* disappear."

He bolted off his bed and lunged at her but then halted and gave her his strange glare. She jerked backward as if someone had yanked on her braids and stumbled into the hall. Gracie's double stood right next to her. She was speechless.

"I can't believe we're twins." He slapped the door shut.

The Past-Gracie's voice muffled through the door. "Me either. I'm glad we're nothing alike, and I'm glad you're grounded." Her voice trailed off as she stomped down the stairs and disappeared from sight. "At least I have common sense." Her voice trailed off.

The scene vanished before them, and Kristian and Gracie stood staring at each other, speechless. They had treated each other awful.

"We acted like total brats," Gracie said.

Kristian shook his head. "This was nothing but a wild goose chase." He stormed out of the house toward the forest, Gracie on his heels.

SanDorak screamed and dove toward them. They both ducked down in the heather. Kristian noticed the veiled light near Alon. "Come on, we have to get to that tree."

TWENTY-SIX

They slid to a halt at the forest's edge, out of sight from SanDorak, but the shadow loomed in front of them.

"This way." Kristian grabbed Gracie's wrist and yanked her along just outside the forest wall.

"Get them," a voice resounded.

"It's Malakon on SanDorak." He raced through the heather, dragging her behind until they reached a clearing. The river roared as it rushed through the forest. "We have to get across."

"But, you can't sw—"

He tugged her until they reached the river. It roared as the cold rush of water swirled around their legs. They crept through the waist-high current. Sharp rocks poked the bottom of his feet. He prayed the current wouldn't suck them under.

SanDorak screamed, and the shadow screeched.

Kristian gripped his sister's hand tighter as they fought to reach the other side. Their wet clothes clung to them, making it harder to move. By the time they reached the other side, Gracie had to haul him up the steep bank.

"I can't go any farther. I need to rest."

"We can't stop. We're almost there." He couldn't imagine where he had gotten his second wind. With wobbly legs, they struggled toward the tree.

"After them." Malakon's voice echoed.

The shadow shrieked, twisted, and hurled around the trees. Its stench whipped through the air. Kristian's legs grew weaker, but he kept going with Gracie in tow.

When the shadow screeched again just as they reached the tree, he clutched her hand. "Jump!"

They jumped into Alon's opening and dropped straight down.

Another shriek told them the shadow had followed them. The sour odor rushed past them. Suddenly, they turned and slid down through another chamber. They heard the sound of a boulder sliding above them.

"Hold on." Kristian grunted as they both slid down a channel until they landed on the ground with a thud. His ankle twisted on his good foot when he hit the ground. His foot throbbed as he rolled from the tree and rammed into something plump.

"Sirus?" He rubbed his foot.

"Uh, huh."

"Where are we?"

"On Dia, by the Great Tree in the valley."

He looked around.

"Thank goodness you're both back safely." Elliott landed and stumbled to a halt. "Let's go." He scooped up all three of them and raced back to the castle. "Did you find the key?"

"No, it was nothing more than a wild goose chase. We ended up on Earth. We didn't find a key. And we barely made it to Alon with our lives." He brushed his hair off his forehead. "Malakon and SanDorak showed up. I have no idea what they were doing there. It seemed like a trap."

Elliott landed in the courtyard. The children slid off. The big stallion nibbled Sirus's tail and swung him to the ground where he landed on his stomach with his legs sprawled. The donkey got to his hooves and glared at Elliott.

Sirus glanced at Kristian. "Are you sure it was a waste of your time?"

"We ended up at our house and had to witness the horrible fight between me and Gracie."

"Yeah, and we acted more like spoiled, rotten brats...and then—" Gracie stopped, and she and Kristian stared at one another. Kristian thought they had acted more like savages. It had been eye-opening.

Sabrina walked up with Gwen, Ruben, and Linnea.

"I know we were gone a long time," Kristian said, "but you'll never guess where we—"

Gwen interrupted him. "You've only been gone a few minutes."

The twins gawked at each other. "That's impossible."

"After you two disappeared inside the tree, we came straight this way and saw Elliott landing in the courtyard with you two. Did you find the tree? The key? What happened?" Gwen twisted her hands and slid off Sabrina.

"We ended up back home, Mom. We didn't find the key. All

we found was SanDorak, the shadow, and…" Kristian glanced at Ruben. "And we either ran into Malakon or…you."

"I assure you it wasn't me," he said. "I've been here the whole time."

Gwen glanced at Ruben. "But where'd you go when you left us at the forest?"

"I wanted to make sure they got to the tree safely."

Kristian and Gracie eyed each other.

***

The planet grew darker as Kristian hobbled inside the castle to the white book. He flipped through the pages. He had never felt such an urgency to find some clues. It was as if a war raged inside of him, and he was running out of time.

Sirus climbed up three steps beside the black pedestal where the book lay. He stretched his neck and rested his snout on top of Kristian's arm like a lazy dog.

"Do you mind? I'm in a hurry here."

"There."

"What?"

"You'll need that." It was a picture of a golden shield.

"For what? I'm not fighting anybody. I'm looking for a key."

Sirus waddled back down the small steps and toward the castle doors. "Follow me."

Kristian followed him outside. Mikal stood with his hands on his hips.

"The key please," Sirus urged.

Mikal glared at them. He yanked the key off his key ring and placed it between Sirus's teeth.

"Comf whif me, Kris-than." Sirus led him down a narrow stairwell to another room below the castle. "Take thith key and unlock the door."

Kristian slipped the key from Sirus's mouth, unlocked the door, and nudged it open. The room was warm. The faint glow of a candle wiggled across the mosaic tile. A shield leaned against the wall beside an armored suit.

"Take that shield."

He surveyed the shield.

"Our enemies want to destroy us, to deceive us. They want us to doubt what is right. This shield will protect you from their fiery darts."

Kristian couldn't understand how this was supposed to happen. He peered at the jumbled letters on the inside of the shield. "What do these letters mean?"

"Follow me."

He followed Sirus back to the courtyard where Mikal paced. The man's hair stuck out like porcupine quills, and his eyes were bloodshot and swollen. He gritted his teeth, sneered at Kristian, and scowled as he flicked his head toward the forest.

"Do you really think you can conquer that beast?"

"What do you know of the creature?" Kristian glared at him.

"Enough to know that a little kid like you won't destroy it. It's a shame you never got to meet your grandfather."

He clenched his teeth. "What do you mean?"

"Good ol' King Aaron. I was his most devoted servant. Unbeknownst to us, however, King Aaron decided to favor Ruben more than Malakon or me. So, Malakon and I devised a— well, let's just say, everything was going according to plan until you showed up." He snarled.

Kristian's chest twinged in spasms, lasting only a few seconds.

"That's enough, Mikal," Sirus said.

"I'm the one who loved your mother, not them. But Aaron ruined everything."

He rushed toward Mikal, but Sirus stepped in front of him. He tumbled over him and landed on his back. "What'd you do that for?"

"We're running out of time. Come along."

"Give me the heart," Mikal shouted.

"Stay away from me." Kristian's hands trembled. "What happened to my grandfather?"

Mikal drew his sword. It looked like gold foil, and he jabbed it at Kristian. "En Garde!"

Kristian jumped back, his shield shaking in his hands. Mikal jabbed the sword, this time hitting his shield. Kristian drew his sword, which wobbled as he parried the best as he could before he stumbled and fell.

"Some swordsman you are, you clumsy ditz." Mikal riposted. The veiled light appeared behind him.

Kristian squeezed the sword's handle and swayed from side to side. He jumped forward and jabbed at him then retreated to his previous position. Mikal jumped toward him, and both swords scraped together. After several minutes, Kristian managed to flip the man's sword out of his hand.

Mikal bolted toward him. They lost their balance and tumbled down the hill, over dry blades of grass that scraped and stung Kristian's arms. After rolling to a stop, he wrapped his legs around Mikal's chest and squeezed as hard as he could. He didn't want to hurt him, but he had to contain him.

But he broke Kristian's grip from his legs. He had no choice than to kick the man's groin. Mikal doubled over, and Kristian ran toward the stables.

"I almost had the heart in the grip of my hand that day by the lake," Mikal shouted after him.

Kristian halted when he reached the stables. "You were on SanDorak that day my dad disappeared."

"James tossed the heart so no one would find it." Mikal's eyes looked like black stones. "But you did."

Kristian's heart palpitated, and he took deep breaths. Mikal lunged, but a hand grabbed his arm and twisted it behind his back. He winced.

"Seems I was there that day too, Mikal."

He stared at Ruben, who clenched his teeth and yanked Mikal's arm higher. "I was hiding behind Alon. I watched the whole incident."

"But—" A thousand thoughts raced through Kristian's mind as he recalled that day.

"James tossed me the heart, but I missed," Ruben said. "He

disappeared into Alon to escape SanDorak. When I heard you coming, Kristian, I hid behind a tree. I never did find the heart."

Kristian slipped his hand inside his pocket and uncurled his fingers in front of Mikal's face. The heart glistened. "Here. Take it, if you want it so bad."

Mikal's eyes glimmered as he stared at the heart.

"Go on."

"Is this a trick?"

"Listen to me," Ruben said firmly. "My brother deceived all of you. He wants the heart because of the power he thinks it holds."

Mikal's breath quivered. "Don't you think I know that? He doesn't care what's best for us. He only wants what's best for himself."

"Then why are you siding with him?" Ruben asked.

Kristian took a deep breath.

"To get back at you for taking Gwen away." Mikal's shoulders slumped. He stared at Ruben, who sighed, seemingly out of compassion.

"Deceivers never make good leaders," Ruben said, "because they rule with selfish motives. Their world revolves around themselves. They pretend they care about others, but they don't."

Kristian felt a tinge of sorrow for him, but how could anyone be so deceived? Did Mikal have no common sense?

"You've lived inside the castle too long," Ruben said. "The Dians have become like empty shells."

"King Aaron stole our freedom. He acted like we had plenty of it, yet he wanted us to do things his way. He got angry when no one wanted to listen to him any longer."

"Gwen shared in your pain. She loved her father and tried to get him to understand, but when she couldn't convince him to change his ways, the Dians slipped farther into hopelessness. And without hope, people die a slow inward death."

Kristian's stomach curled into a sour knot. His mother had been the Dians' only hope? Until now, the Dians had only been a vague avatar to him. But now, especially since his mother was Dian, he understood them a little better. They had become slaves to fear.

Mikal's pallid face became stoic. He was handsome, with physical strength, but he now appeared frail and defeated—a man without purpose. He hung his head and wandered off aimlessly.

Ruben and Kristian stared at each other. Kristian's heart flicked. He felt a strange feeling when he looked at this man.

TWENTY-SEVEN

The ground trembled, the clouds churned, and the wind carried faint cries across the dusky sky as white mist drifted up through the forest.

Kristian hoisted the strap of his shield farther up on his shoulder and surveyed the land. Feeling a bit more courageous, he rushed into the castle and flipped through the white book again, hoping to find another clue that would make sense of the whole thing. Sirus and the others crowded around him as he stared at a picture of a mustard tree on one of the pages. Gracie peered over his shoulder, breathing spurts of warm air on his neck.

"Back up, would you?" he told her. He glanced at Sirus as thoughts bounced around in his head like a tennis ball trapped in a cube. "I have to find this mustard tree."

Sirus nodded.

A black, rider-less Friesian stallion landed in the courtyard. His coat looked like moist satin, and he stretched his foreleg in a gesture for Kristian to climb up.

"Go on," Elliott said. "This is my brother, Drake. He will see you through the rest of your journey."

Kristian recognized him from the picture in the bunkhouse. "But I want you to go with me."

"It doesn't appear that the darkness is affecting him like it has us, so he is stronger than us. Maybe it's because he and his family live outside the boundaries of Dia in the south. You will be safer with him."

Drake flicked his head.

"Why hasn't it affected you?" he asked Drake.

"I'm not sure, but do not fear, I will protect you."

Kristian nodded, gripped Drake's mane, and climbed up. Drake stood taller than Elliott and Sabrina and built like a warhorse. His shoulders were thick and his muscles tight and more defined then theirs. Kristian took a deep breath and lifted the black leather reins.

Ruben stroked Drake's forehead and looked at Kristian. "I know you're not sure if you can trust me, but you'll see that you can."

Kristian nodded. He glanced at Sirus.

"This is your journey," Sirus said.

"But how do I know where the mustard tree is?"

"Mustard tree?" Ruben asked. "There's a mustard tree by my castle on Lia."

"There is? Then that's it."

"May I come with you?" Linnea stepped forward.

Kristian glanced at Sirus, who nodded. "I'd like that."

"But what about me?" Gracie asked.

He felt confident without her this time. And it felt good. "I think we'll be all right. Why don't you stay here with Mom?"

Linnea climbed up and clung to his waist. Drake galloped into the sky and was soon flying over Dia. He squeezed through the wormhole and out the other side into a sea of stars.

"Take us to Lia," Linnea said.

Kristian's spine tingled. "We're going to that bright planet in the distance?"

"Yes. That's Lia."

As they drew closer to the planet, they had to shield their eyes from the planet's glowing ring.

"Lift your shield." She helped him raise it in front of them. "Duck down."

He hunched behind the shield as Drake burst through the ring and felt a tingling across his body. When he peeked over the shield, he saw a place that looked like a fairytale land.

"This is the place I saw in the white book."

He had fantasized about such a place. There was a bright, white sandstone castle with dozens of towers reaching high into the sky. It sat on a large island in the middle of a huge lake. White-capped mountains stood behind it in the distance, and the lake shimmered from the natural light of the land. The land was spotless; flora and fauna vividly flourished. Ancient creatures roamed the planet freely. It was like a paradise—a place of such beauty and tranquility that he didn't want to leave. He felt so at home here.

Drake glided over the wide river that meandered through the valley where it emptied into the lake. A mighty oak grew near the river's mouth, and near the lake was a long bridge that stretched across to the castle.

They landed with elegance on a courtyard that was inlaid with gold. Drake's hooves spattered as he stepped closer to the drawbridge.

Kristian scanned every inch of the castle. His heart fluttered when he found the mustard tree. It was at least twenty feet high. Its crooked trunk and bent branches grew helter-skelter into the air, but it was the most interesting tree he had ever seen.

They slid off the Friesian. Kristian hobbled up to the tree and touched its thick, shiny, oval leaves.

"A mustard tree has tiny seeds," Linnea said. "It's hard to imagine they can grow to such heights."

"Almost unimaginable," he whispered and looked around. "This place is so awesome."

She grappled with her thick, wavy hair and flipped it behind her shoulders. "It's Malakon's and Ruben's birth planet."

"Where is everybody?"

"That's another story for later. The only ones here are those in Ruben's army. They keep the place tidy." She pointed to the base of a mountain where the stables were. They were huge and built with a thick, light gray wood and trimmed in white that sparkled in the light.

"Do you know anything about the jewel box?"

"No, sorry." Her hair sprayed around her shoulders.

"It has to be here. I think the key to the golden heart might be inside of it."

"Then we should waste no more time. Let's search."

They crept inside the empty castle, through the foyer, and beneath the dual, heart-shaped staircases that curved up both sides toward the second floor. They slinked down the maroon runner that led across a dark sienna, marble floor to a throne room with a ribbed ceiling that looked like the keel of a ship.

Three stairs led to an apse, and inside the semi-circular, vaulted room sat a throne of fine quality with a blue velvet seat. A tapestry hung on the wall behind the throne, made of red and green silk and trimmed in gold. Painted on the wall across from the tapestry was a mural of twelve men dressed in long, white robes, standing around a bearded man, who was dressed the same.

"This way." He crept past four white, marble columns that looked just like the ones he'd seen in the white book. Beyond the columns, inside a small alcove, was a mural consisting of a forest, a river, a waterfall, and a large oak tree. Painted on the ceiling were images of the moon, several planets, and hundreds of twinkling stars.

Goosebumps crawled across Kristian's arms as he scanned the room. "Look."

He spotted a gold desk and scooted toward it. He reached for the knob of the drawer and slid it open. His eyes widened when he saw a jewel box covered with diamonds. He took a deep breath and glanced at Linnea.

She nodded. "Ruben's father gave him that when he was young after telling him he was to be the next king of Lia."

"How do you know this?"

"Ruben told me. He said he and Mikal used to play together when they were small and had become best friends. But after Mikal's parents died, Ruben said Mikal had withdrawn into his own world and wanted nothing to do with anybody."

"But why does Malakon insist that he's the king of Dia?"

"Dia and Lia are twin planets, formed at the same time. Ruben is actually king of both, but Malakon is only interested in Dia."

"Why?"

"His and Ruben's mother is buried here."

Linnea's words drifted past him as he stared at the box.

"Well, what are you waiting for? Open it."

He slipped the key that he had taken from Ruben's box into the tiny keyhole. He closed his eyes, took a deep breath, and turned the key with a click. But before he had a chance to open the lid, hooves thumped onto the courtyard.

His eyes widened. "What was that?"

Linnea dashed to the door. "It's Malakon. He's in the courtyard, coming this way," she said, scrambling back to Kristian. "But I don't see Drake. He must be in the back. I'll meet you there. Hurry."

He lifted the lid, and there, nestled on top of light blue velvet was a tiny, silver key. "The key!"

The castle doors burst open as Malakon sprinted toward him. "You led me right to it like I knew you would."

Kristian shoved the key into his pocket and hobbled at a quick pace through the castle and out the back where Drake and Linnea waited.

"Stop," Malakon shouted.

As soon as Kristian's feet left the ground, Drake was in the air and speeding through the glowing blue light toward Dia where Elliott and the others were waiting in the courtyard.

Kristian was halfway down Drake's mane, shouting, "I found it," when he lost his balance and tripped, scraping his hand. A burning sensation pounded on the wound.

Gwen whimpered and rushed to help him up. "You found it. After all these years."

He opened the diamond box. Gwen clutched her heart as she stared at the key. "Oh, thank goodness."

"It's time," Sirus said. "We must go now." Darkness was falling fast.

Kristian brought his trembling hand to his forehead and stared at his mother's expression. He'd never seen her so excited. "Sirus…please, come with me this time. You have to."

"I'll need to stay—"

"Drake." Kristian wasn't listening to his excuses this time.

The big horse plucked Sirus off the ground quicker than a leaping frog and dropped him on top of his back.

"I'm coming too," Gracie said.

"No, not this time."

She clapped her hands. "Drake."

Drake scooped her up and dropped her between Sirus and Linnea.

Kristian shook his head. "I said no."

"Too late."

His mom touched his arm. "Understand that the shadow represents our fears. Only faith can destroy our fears."

He nodded, even though he didn't quite understand it all, and then scrambled up onto Drake in front of the others. He grabbed the reins, and they raced through the sky. Kristian turned and glanced back at his mom, knowing he may never see her again. He felt bad for being so angry with her—it wasn't her fault she'd acted as she had.

The forest looked like a giant, dark glob, but the boundary was still slightly visible. It wouldn't be long before the boundaries would vanish entirely and meld into the darkness, setting the shadow loose.

Kristian spotted the veiled light over the forest. This time he decided to listen. "That way, straight ahead." He kept his eye on the veiled light as Drake sped over the forest.

"You do realize we're headed for the Valley of the Shadow of Death?" Drake's voice shuddered.

"The Valley of w-what?" Kristian felt the Friesian's copious muscles quiver beneath him.

"Your faith is about to be tested," Sirus said.

He had little faith and wondered if it would be enough to succeed at the task before him.

Cool, windy gusts pushed against them, and a strong, bitter odor stung his nostrils. He squeezed his fingers around Drake's reins.

Drake's throat rattled, and it sounded like a growl. Kristian had never heard a horse growl until now. Sweat seeped from the stallion's coat and gleamed from the vague light of the wormhole. The sky was a dismal, dark blueberry. Emerald green, fluorescent lights blinked like lightning bugs through the dusk, giving off enough light to light their way.

"What if—" Kristian began, but Sirus interrupted him.

"No what ifs. Do not allow the shadow to intimidate you. It'll sense your fear and lead to our death."

Gracie whimpered and shook.

Kristian took a deep breath and slipped his hand on top of his hilt then realized the sword was useless against this creature. He slipped his hand into his pocket and clasped the golden heart instead.

Linnea whispered. "You can do this."

He took a deep breath. The shadow screamed.

"Stop." Malakon's voice echoed through the sky. "Do not destroy that creature. It belongs to me. If I cannot be king, then Dia will fail to exist."

"Go, Drake." Linnea wrapped her arms around Kristian's waist and squeezed Sirus. "Don't listen to him."

Kristian's heart quivered. Sirus wheezed as Drake raced through the forest, whipping branches along the way. Soon, they passed the forest wall and into the Valley of the Shadow of Death in the middle of the forest. Hundreds of snake-like shadows with orange eyes darted their red tongues and danced across the foggy valley floor.

TWENTY-EIGHT

Kristian leaned forward giving Drake full rein. He whispered to Drake, "Can you see the light?"

"Yes."

"I figured you could. Follow it."

Drake raised his head and raced like a cheetah through the dark valley. Shadows moved swiftly on both sides to keep pace with them through the forest. Drake slowed to a stop and landed on the valley floor without making a sound. They all slid off and tiptoed behind Kristian. Linnea took a stance, her bow and arrow fixed on the surrounding area.

The shadow's hot, stinging breath drifted toward them. Its menacing, pulsating eye appeared in the forest, casting a green glow on the trees. Kristian could see its blood-red mouth opened wide through the trees. He stood, frozen. When he turned, he couldn't see the others.

"Where is everybody?"

Someone grabbed his arm and dragged him into a pitch-black tunnel under ground. "What's going on?"

The mystery person shushed him and shoved a large, round object over a hole. "This way."

Kristian peered through the darkness. "Mikal? What are you doing here?"

"Just follow me."

"But what about Drake?"

"He'll be waiting for us at the other end of this tunnel. Your other friends are here too."

They made their way down the damp tunnel toward the other end, with Kristian dragging his shield behind him.

"Quiet," Linnea said. "I think the shadow's at the other end."

A growl made its way down the tunnel. They turned the other way and hustled back. Sweat rolled into Kristian's eyes. He could barely see ahead of him. When they finally exited the tunnel, they discovered a planet out of control. It went from hot, to cold, to a windstorm, to snow flurries, to sleet, and then rain—and then started the cycle all over again.

"We must move quickly," Sirus said.

Drake swooped down and plucked them up with a set of his wings. "Glad we found you, Mikal." The shadow swept in behind them.

"Uh oh." Sirus quivered.

The veiled light appeared like a flame that raced in front of them.

"Follow it." Kristian looked back at the shadow.

"Follow what?" Gracie asked.

A curtain of darkness had finally devoured the planet.

"The forest boundaries—they're gone!" Kristian's heart pounded. The only light they had now was the light from the veiled light's burning flame.

Mikal's voice shook. "Now what do we do?"

"We have to get the shadow to chase us," Kristian said.

"Great idea," Linnea said.

"Are you out of your mind?" Gracie asked.

He gripped the reins. "We have to lure the shadow through the wormhole."

"Again, are you out of your mind? We'll be trapped out in space with that monster."

For the first time ever, Kristian felt like he had a good and sensible idea. He hoped it would work. The squiggly dark creatures on the valley floor stood like walking canes, stretched toward the sky, but they didn't pursue them.

Drake swept through the Valley of the Shadow of Death and headed toward the wormhole. Kristian pinched the glowing, golden heart and held it in the air hoping the shadow would follow. The green eye dipped in behind them, screaming louder than Kristian had heard.

"Here it comes." He grasped the heart tighter as Drake sped up. "Hang on, everyone!" Kristian gripped the shield's bar just as they slipped inside the wormhole and out into the universe. Frosty air whistled past them. Kristian could see the slight outlines of the swirling wind.

Sirus shook, and Gracie shivered. But Linnea remained calm. Cosmic lightning zigzagged across the heavens in a sea of storms. Kristian trembled at the cosmic ordeal before him. A giant vortex of purple and blue gasses whipped toward them, growing louder the closer it came. Mikal's pale face shimmered from sweat. Electrical charges arced, sending solar flares crisscrossing through the universe as if a fireworks outlet store blew up. The booms throbbed in Kristian's ears.

"Look." Gracie pointed. The outer cosmos sucked matter into a massive vortex, consuming every heavenly body in its path.

"The universe is out of control." Kristian's voice cracked through the explosions.

Clusters of lights popped as the vortex broke into two colossal twisters, headed straight toward the cosmic vortex. Comets and shooting stars zipped past helter-skelter. Gazillions of neon lights squirreled through space as electromagnetic beams split the universe.

Kristian jerked his head to the side. There it was—the foreboding green eye had now grown into a monstrous proportion as it sucked the blackness into its body.

He struggled to raise his shield through the gusts. As he managed to draw his sword, he wriggled his thumb to the pommel. With a click, the sword's emerald laser shot from the tip of the sword. It slashed through the darkness as he struggled to get it under control. The shadow's eye went berserk, as if the laser confused it.

Gracie buried her face in her hands. "I can't look. No, I mean—let m-me help."

She reached for Kristian's sword, but Linnea clutched her wrist and shook her head.

"Can't you see he needs me?" Gracie screamed. "Let go."

"I shall not. Leave him be."

"You're trying to kill us." Gracie jerked her hand back, but Linnea squeezed tighter. Then with her other hand, Gracie took hold of

Kristian's jittery arm, causing the laser to shoot back and forth.

"Stop it," Kristian scolded her, and she let go.

Drake spread a set of his wings over them to protect them from flying space debris, as the wind grew stronger. The shadow spun faster like a black twister. The stallion dashed to the right, but the shadow swirled that way. He zipped back to the left, but the shadow followed.

Kristian slashed the laser through the shadow, but it didn't faze it, except that its malicious, green eye turned red. Its face appeared like an ancient, wrinkled man.

"I don't understand how faith will save us," Kristian murmured, and then raising his voice, he screamed, "I. Choose. Faith!"

Immediately, a blinding light burst from Lia. The light was so intense that the stars temporarily vanished. The shadow stopped spinning and froze like a black statue. Everything stopped, and the silence was deafening. The blinding light circled the shadow. Kristian shook until his body felt like tremors.

"D-don't waver. Faith w-will protect and shield you from your enemies." Sirus trembled.

Kristian's entire body convulsed as the sword wobbled in his grip.

"Look." Gracie pointed.

Racing toward them was an army of translucent, snow-white Friesians, pulling chariots of fire with flaming wheels. To Kristian's astonishment, Ruben led them.

The chariots circled the shadow in a wide birth, trapping it inside a blazing ring. The shadow screamed, gyrated, twirled, and swirled. Its eye flashed red and rolled all around in the top half of its body.

Ruben drew his chariot up beside them. "Get on."

Kristian glanced at Sirus, who nodded. Ruben helped him scramble into his chariot. Kristian had second thoughts. "Come on, Gracie."

Just as Gracie swung her leg over the side to step in with him, Linnea stopped her again.

"Stop it." Gracie tugged her leg away from Linnea's grip.

"You need to stop babying him."

She leered at Linnea. Kristian licked his lips and nodded at his sister, who begrudgingly relented by jerking away and handed him his shield.

"Not only must you fulfill your mother's destiny, you are a direct descendant of King Aaron, and you are predestined to become Dia's new king." Linnea glanced at him. He felt lightheaded at this bit of news. "Now hurry."

The shadow's screeches stirred him back to reality. Gracie looked horrified.

Kristian gripped the sword. "Okay, let's go."

"Only the true King of Dia can open the golden heart," Ruben said. "Your mother had sensed it all along, but now you must have the faith of a mustard seed for any of this to work."

"So you knew all along?"

"Yes."

The shadow screamed. Linnea glanced at Kristian as Ruben

tried to keep his steed from bolting. She pointed to her chest. "Believe. You are not alone. This is your moment in time."

He nodded. She was right; he felt it. He stared at the shadowy beast and took a deep breath. His chest swelled, and he gripped the shield. Deep red liquid oozed from the shadow's eye and trailed down its murky, twisted form.

"Stay away from it." Malakon's voice echoed. A great army of warriors rode behind him.

"Stay back." Ruben raised his sword. Half of Ruben's chariots broke from the circle and formed a fiery wall between them and Malakon's army, whose restless steeds stopped. Ruben said, "The time is now."

Kristian bit his bottom lip. The thunder of chariots pounded in his ears as they sped in a continuous circle around the shadow.

"We'll pass over the ring of fire. Then you must do the rest."

"But how do I know when to throw it?"

"You'll know," Ruben said.

A ball of mucus stuck in Kristian's throat, and the sword shook in his hands. He raised his shield. A blinding blaze of light from Lia broke through Lia's cupola and shot through the universe toward him. The light exploded onto the back of the shield, temporarily blinding him. He closed his eyes and could still see the light sparking through his eyelids.

When the light fizzled, he peeked at his shield. His mouth fell open when letters appeared on the inside of the shield.

"Shout those words," Sirus called.

Kristian moved his lips, but the words wouldn't come. The shadow loomed larger over them. Ruben fought to keep the reins tight on his steed.

"I-eld-Sh—fo—ith-Fa!" As soon as Kristian spoke the last syllable of the last word, the letters unscrambled and glowed, spelling out 'Shield of Faith.'

"Shield of Faith," he shouted. "This shield…it's the shield of faith!" His adrenaline hit high alert, and he thought his heart would burst out of his chest. He gripped the shield and raised it high in the air. "I choose faith!"

Kristian jiggled the key into the keyhole of the golden heart. The shadow darted around as Ruben edged his steed closer to it. It swirled and screamed like a hundred wounded animals. He shook so hard that he could barely keep his hand steady long enough to put the key in the hole and unlock the heart as the shadow bore down on top of them.

Ruben struggled with the reins. "Kristian!"

He squealed as he tried to hit the hole. He glanced up and noticed the veiled light above them. It had shed its veil and appeared larger than life, shining as bright as a hundred shiny rubies.

The shadow moved in and opened its deadly mouth.

Kristian attempted to put the key in the hole again. This time it worked. The key clicked in the lock, and the golden heart popped open. Breathless, Kristian stared at the treasured morsel that had lain hidden for generations. The luminous Heart of Pearl was nestled on a bed of rich, apple-red velvet.

Kristian pinched the tiny, flawless Heart of Pearl and held tight. The shadow thrashed about like a caged animal. Then it stopped and hooked its neck like a cobra.

"Light and darkness cannot coexist." Kristian's words echoed throughout the universe.

The shadow opened its red mouth in shuddering screams.

He threw the Heart of Pearl into the creature's mouth, and the pearl burst into a huge flame as it spiraled down the dark chamber to its bowels. The shadow gagged, choked, writhed, and convulsed. Its eye spun out of control.

Ruben and Kristian raced back over the chariot's fiery circle.

When the Heart of Pearl reached the bottom of the creature's bowels, the shadowy creature burst into trillions of embers that sprayed across the universe. Kristian watched until they drifted from sight.

The universe was once again at peace. They caught their breath as they inhaled the silence.

"Kristian, you did it!" Gracie shouted, as she jumped up and down.

"You'll all regret this." Malakon's voice cut through the silence as he shook his fist. "You'll all be sorry. You don't know what you've done. I warned you."

As he and his army sped out sight, the wormhole expanded to its original size with greater splendor than before.

Kristian glanced at Linnea, who smiled, and he smiled back.

As Kristian and Sirus climbed back on Drake, he noticed a hint of red in Ruben's pupils, but then they returned to normal. He shook his head. Maybe it was just a Dian trait.

"The universe looks so fresh and new," Gracie said as they all headed back to Dia.

"Yeah, it's like the universe has been reborn or something. Look over there." Kristian pointed. It looked like new planets and galaxies forming. He could scarcely take in the sight without losing his breath. He wished everyone on Earth could see such majesty as this.

"I wonder how many times this has happened," his sister said.

"No one knows," Linnea replied. Gracie gave her a withering look. Kristian hoped they could become friends.

Before they reached the wormhole, glittery particles drifted down like fresh snow on the first day of winter. If there was such a substance as moon dust, Kristian was sure this was it. He inhaled the joyful peace.

TWENTY-NINE

A few weeks later, the planet began to restore itself. The river turned back into a deep blue, shimmering beneath the bright, glimmering rays of a lemon sun. A myriad of flowers dotted the landscape, and rich green grass blew in the breeze. The rainbow over the castle had found new life and exploded into a kaleidoscope of brilliant colors.

Deer, foxes, big-horned sheep, and all kinds of creatures meandered the mountainsides and in the valley. The wind whistled along the slopes as the waterfalls gushed over the cliffs, plundering into the frothy-tipped lake. The scent of 'everything that was right' danced in the wind. The Dians resurfaced and were hard at work tidying up their neglected homesteads, while talking cheerfully with their neighbors and catching up on the past events.

They looked oddly similar, yet each had their own physical flaw just like Kristian. Did his mom, Ruben, or even Sabrina have a flaw that he hadn't noticed? And what about Gracie? He couldn't find anything physically wrong with her—yet.

The Dians seemed as if they were beginning to regain their strength, including him and Gracie. He and Gracie had somehow established an unusual aura about them, too, like the others. But he decided that they didn't really look like Dians because they'd grown up on Earth.

The Dians needed help trusting people again, especially another king.

Kristian found a nice spot on the bank of the river to ponder the events that occurred over the past few weeks. He fiddled with his foot and wondered what the future held. His heart fluttered at the thought that he and Gracie were part of a royal family. And had his mom really known the difference between Ruben and Malakon?

Ruben at least tried to make time for him and Gracie these last few weeks, making an effort to get to know them better. He hated to admit it yet, but he liked Ruben and could understand why his mom had fallen in love with him. He had displayed total affection toward her; whenever he looked at her it was as if he was in another world— the same with her when she looked at him. He wished she wouldn't have kept such secrets from them, but he could understand why. And it wasn't Ruben's fault.

Kristian sighed. How could he and Gracie ever really know who their father was for sure?

He thought about how the golden heart had protected the Heart of Pearl all those years, and he couldn't help but think about how the human body protects human hearts.

The Pippins flitted overhead, following Meme as she sung and frolicked in the air. She saluted him. "Sir."

"Hi, Meme," he replied, giving her a salute.

Someone cleared his throat next to Kristian, and he looked down. He hadn't heard Sirus sit beside him. The little donkey glanced up at him with half-moon lids. His grin, as usual, revealed purple teeth. Kristian flicked a speck of a blueberry off the corner of his friend's mouth.

"Blueberries again, I see." He grinned.

"What can I say?" Sirus rolled over, flicked his hooves in the air, and wiggled his back in the grass.

He scratched his stomach. "Someday I may not be around to scratch you, you know."

A hoof accidentally socked his chest, and he fell backward. "Ouch!"

"Oops." Sirus rolled over and they frolicked in the grass before Sirus stood up. "Sorry."

Kristian sat up and hugged his knees. He gazed at the gently flowing river. "Thanks for all your help. I don't know what I would've done without you."

When Sirus didn't answer him, he looked down and found that his friend was gone. All that remained was a crumpled envelope left in the impression of Sirus's butt on the ground.

Elliott cleared his throat. "And you are talking to...who?"

"I was talking to— Did you see Sirus?" Kristian picked up the envelope and slipped the letter out. The first three words he read caused his heart to quiver.

"My Dearest Grandson, I only recently discovered that I had two grandchildren. And twins at that! You can imagine my joy. Sabrina snitched and told me everything, although your mother never knew it. I wanted to tell you and your sister that our destinies depend on the choices we make. Choices decide our life's path. I hope that my daughter, your mother, will one day know of an old man's changed heart and my regrets. I want her to know that I took her advice and granted the Dians their freedom after all."

Kristian grinned as he tried to imagine his grandfather. He continued reading.

"Sabrina confessed to me that Ruben is Gwen's husband, and your and Gracie's father. In the event that something happens to me, please tell Ruben that the throne and the Kingdom of Dia, indeed, belong to him. Gwen and James have been gone far too long from Dia, and I had to make a decision. I had no idea if they would return. And please tell him that Malakon threatened my dear Gwen's and my life, and this is why I broke my promise to Ramón, Ruben's and Malakon's father."

He wiped the corner of his eye.

"Ruben comforted me, an old man, after Gwen left Dia, and I am thankful he did. Therefore, if fate calls me from this life before I've a chance to look on your and your sister's faces or to tell your mother how sorry I am, please, will you give her this letter? I hope you don't think less of me."

The last few lines blurred.

"I wait anxiously to meet you both. Your most loving grandfather, King Aaron."

Kristian folded the splotched letter and wiped his nose on his sleeve. He stared at the blurry blades of grass, and hated that his mom had kept all of this from him. He flinched when someone touched his shoulder.

"Please, come with me," Gwen said. Sabrina flew her, Kristian, and Gracie to the underground cavern that housed the sphere. Inside the sphere, a scene appeared.

A handsome man stood in the picture, wearing a white shirt beneath a tan parlor coat and dark brown pants. He paced in front of a girl who appeared to be in her late teens. He stopped in front of a mirror and straightened the copper crown on his head.

"Daughter, why would you—" the king began, but the girl interrupted.

"I'm not a child. I want to experience Earth like you and mother did."

Kristian's mouth slipped open. "That's you and grandfather?"

Gwen nodded.

"Wow!" Gracie brushed her fingers across the sphere as if she hoped to touch him.

King Aaron reached for his daughter's hand with trembling fingers. "If you go, my dear, you may not be able to return to Dia."

The girl's face grew solemn. "But why? You and mother went and returned."

The king strolled to a window and clasped his hands behind his back. "I am afraid that if you leave, it will appear as if you are publicly declaring your dissatisfaction with me and my kingdom, which would bring dishonor upon me."

"That's not my plan at all, but…but if you don't allow it, I shall go anyway." She turned away and folded her arms.

He reached into his pocket. "Look."

She spun around, and he unfolded his fingers.

"The golden heart." Kristian flicked his eyes at his mom, who nodded.

The scene continued. "I found this beside the Great Tree in the valley," the king told his daughter. "I believe it has some kind of power."

"What makes you think so?"

"I believe this was the only object that allowed your mother and I to return to Dia."

Her eyes brightened. "Then give it to me, so I may go to Earth too, and then I will return safely."

The king frowned. "Earth is not a safe place right now. There is a strange and terrible creature that roams about."

Kristian's eyes widened. He and Gracie both whispered, "The shadow."

The king pleaded with his daughter. "Everything you need is right here. Why would you want to go?"

"I am more afraid to stay than to go."

"Why do you say that?"

Young Gwen fumbled with her fingers. "A genuine king would not call any kingdom *his* kingdom, but rather, *the people's*. Have you not gazed at the Dians' faces? They are void of hope, expressionless. You've stolen their independence and freedom, as well as mine. We are not here for your pleasure, or for you to rule over us."

The king clutched his chest and wheezed. He reached for his

daughter's hand and placed the golden heart in her palm. "Go, then. Take this with you, but guard it with your life."

The scene faded.

"Your grandfather believed he was doing what was best for us, but he was blind to the truth. Dictatorship is not thrilling. He robbed us of joy and burdened our lives." Gwen dabbed the corner of her eye with her knuckle. "Even so, I miss him."

Kristian spoke softly. "You didn't give us a chance to know our grandparents. Grandfather was a king. How awesome is that? We're royalty, and we never knew it, never got to experience it."

"Yeah," Gracie said, "Dia is our heritage too." She placed her hands on her hips. "You kept that from us."

Gwen's bottom lip quivered. "I'm sorry. My greatest regret is that I made mistakes, and I can't go back in time and change anything. But Earth was worth taking the chance on. It's a special place; one of the grandest of all the planets because its people are different. They were created with loving and kind spirits, and they have the freedom to live their lives however they choose." She fumbled with her dress. "That's what I wanted for Dia—what I wanted for you.

"Ruben is a wonderful man. I hope you'll give him a chance. His angelic smile lights up my world." She sighed. "And it still does after all these years. None of this was his fault. My father didn't trust him, so he forbade me to see him. He was devastated when he discovered that Ruben's father, King Ramón, had married us.

"Ramón was my father's dearest friend. He made my father promise that if anything should happen to him that he would raise

Ruben and Malakon. Ramón's kingdom belongs to Ruben too, because he is the firstborn. Malakon had become so insanely jealous that he banished him to Zorak, took Ruben against his will."

Kristian saw the distant look on her face once again, but this time, his heart softened because he understood it now. "Are you sure you know the difference between Ruben and Malakon?"

She hesitated. "Of course I do. All you have to do is look at his heart."

He glanced at Gracie, and his stomach flitted. He hoped she was right. "Tell us why the Great Tree in the valley seems so familiar."

"Come."

Sabrina flew them to the Great Tree. Gwen slid off and motioned the children to follow. She strolled beneath some entwining limbs that had taken the shape of a tunnel. Behind the tree, hidden from sight, was a spiral staircase that wound up through the trunk to an alcove. They stepped inside.

They scanned the room. A candle lamp sat unlit on a table made of twigs between two cradles. A rocking chair, made from woven tree limbs, holding faded, overstuffed cushions, sat near the cribs. "This is where you were born."

Kristian and Gracie stood in stunned silence.

"I had to keep you secret. Sabrina discovered Malakon's plot to abduct one of you and later trade you for the golden heart. There was only one thing to do to protect you, and that was to leave Dia. When we were on Earth, I knew you had seen the shadow, Kristian. I figured it must have been after the golden heart. I kept quiet about it so you wouldn't be fearful, but I see that it didn't work. I'll never keep the truth from either of you again."

Time seemed to stand still when he stared into his mom's eyes. And he wouldn't jump to conclusions anymore when he didn't know the truth about things. He realized everyone had a past, some good, and some not so good, but no one was perfect.

Gracie hugged her mom. "We haven't been the best twins a mother could ask for."

"I couldn't have asked for any better than you two." Gwen smiled.

Kristian's eyes watered. "What happened to Dad—I mean, James?"

Gwen shook her head. "I don't know. I miss him so much. And my father. Maybe they will return somehow."

"I'm going to find out what happened to James," Kristian said. "I don't believe he's dead; I have a newfound faith that he is still alive and we'll find him."

He reached for her hand and placed the envelope in it. He gently squeezed her fingers around it and left with his arm around Gracie's shoulder.

***

Gwen's cheeks glistened as she twirled in the courtyard, clutching the envelope to her chest. "Doesn't Dia look all brand new? I've never seen it so lovely. It feels so good to be home."

Kristian grinned. He had never seen her so happy. Ruben strolled over to her, picked her up, and swung her in a circle. Kristian turned. Linnea was brushing one of the Friesians by the stable. He heard Elliott and Sabrina discussing something, so he decided to listen in and pretend he wasn't.

"Time to fess up, bro." Sabrina lowered her brow. "It's time to forgive and go on."

Elliott pressed his nose in the air, swished his tail, and strode off, but she wouldn't leave him alone. She trotted around him and halted. He jerked to a standstill.

"Later." He bumped into her.

"No, we'll talk now."

Elliott gave a subdued grin, and they wandered off down the path. Kristian knew Sabrina had hurt Elliott's feelings by not telling him that she'd taken them to Earth.

THIRTY

Kristian hobbled to the riverbank to look for Sirus. The little donkey was the only one who knew about the veiled light besides him and was the first one he'd met when he'd arrived on Dia. He threw a clump of grass into the river and watched as it swirled downstream. He smelled a rose fragrance in the air and knew it was Linnea.

"Did you know that a week on Dia is a year on Earth?" she asked.

Kristian stared at her. "No way."

"Yeah. It's the whole hyperspace-wormhole philosophy or some such thing."

Kristian could hardly imagine it. "So you mean years have passed on Earth since I've been here?"

Linnea nodded. He gave it a little more thought but then wondered where Sirus could have wandered off to. "You wouldn't know where Sirus is, would you?"

"His job is finished here, at least for now."

"What do you mean?"

"He came here because of you. The golden heart protected the Heart of Pearl, which had been created for this moment in time, as were you."

Kristian listened intently.

"We all have a heart of pearl inside of us for when we need it. It can sometimes shine like the sun when we need it in a dark world. But we have to ignite the flame and yield to the process if we want it to work properly. We must guard our hearts so they will become a living well in our lives."

A large, bluish-green fish jumped out of the water and splashed with a *plunk.* A flock of bluebirds the color of the South Pacific flittered overhead, chirping melodiously, showing off their orange breasts and white stomachs.

"Even the smallest of seeds contain life," she continued, "as you know from the mustard seed. And now, you have the seed of faith and can see things more clearly."

Kristian gazed over the river as her words circled in his mind. It was as if he could listen to her talk all day, which wasn't normal, but…he had to find Sirus.

The grass rustled. Linnea walked away, and Gracie took her place.

"Have you seen Sirus?" he asked.

Gracie shrugged. "No. Not to change the subject, but Linnea is so weird. She hasn't one ounce of tomboy in her. She's so ladylike until there's danger. Then she turns into this mighty warrior-type and who-knows-what else."

"It wouldn't hurt you to take a lesson from her. Not every girl likes acting like a boy, you know. Some girls like to be a lady and be treated like one."

"I don't act like a boy all the time. I'm still a girl, you know."

She smirked.

"I like her." He put his hands on his hips and scanned the mountainside across the river before hobbling up the riverbank.

"Sirus will show up at some point," Gracie called over her shoulder. "He always does. Where can he go?"

Yes, where could he go? And what was he up to? He had a sinking feeling in the pit of his stomach. He scrambled to the blueberry grove and looked under each bush. He cupped the sides of his mouth and called his name several times.

A movement caught his eye high on a cliff beneath a large dogwood tree. Sirus stood next to the veiled light, which was now veilless and in the shape of a glowing, red heart. There was a stranger standing next to them, who appeared to be a man. His presence was brilliant.

The red heart floated away and, with it, the presence of the stranger. Sirus stared at Kristian for a long while before turning and wobbling away.

"Don't leave," he called. A hand touched his shoulder as he tried to catch his breath.

"You still have me, you know," Gracie said.

He turned and waited for her to start laughing. But she didn't.

"No matter what, nothing or no one can weaken the blood of twins."

When he realized she was serious, his heart was full. He turned the corner of his mouth into a grin.

***

Dusk fell over the land as Lia's light dimmed. Night was falling. Kristian had learned that Lia was the light that lit Dia. His journey was over, his mother's destiny fulfilled. He took a deep breath and sighed.

The smell of lilacs drifted through the air. Kristian heard a dog yelp.

Was he hearing things? He hadn't seen one dog since he'd been here. The dog yelped again. He turned toward the sound.

A dog sprang from Gwen's arms and raced toward him. "Nick!"

Nick yelped and leaped into Kristian's arms, knocking him down. The dog slobbered all over his face, wagging his tail tirelessly, and licking Kristian's chin vigorously.

He sat up and noticed Linnea out of the corner of his eye, sitting beneath a blooming cherry tree. She giggled, and he smiled. Nick bounded from Kristian's lap, raced toward her, and jumped on her lap.

"Hey, get back here." He laughed.

Just then, Gracie rushed across the courtyard, tripping along the way, and shouting. "Kristian! Mom!"

Kristian thought her lungs would burst.

"You'll never believe it. My book—*my* white book... It's arrived. It replaced yours, Kristian. Now I have one!"

~A heartfelt thank you to all of you who answered my many questions in the process of bringing this story to life. I know you know who you are.